ALL IN THE FAMILY

Ruff Justice's brother Roland had loved this girl, Natalie Forrest, and Ruff could see why. The cattle king's daughter stood before him, naked, fire-glossed, her thighs smooth and tapered, breasts jutting, dark-nippled, waist concave and small. Her eyes glistened. Her hands reached out toward Ruff, fingers wiggling impatiently. She looked up at him briefly, then looked downward as she began undoing his belt.

Ruff wanted to say that this wasn't right, not with his brother cold in the grave. But he couldn't tell her he didn't want her, not when her widening eyes looked so longingly at him. He could only do what she wanted ... what he wanted, too ... following his brother's path of pleasure ... heading closer to his brother's bloody fate. . . .

Wild Westerns by Warren T. Longtree

RUFF JUSTICE #16

HIGH VENGEANCE

by
Warren T. Longtree

A SIGNET BOOK

NEW AMERICAN LIBRARY

PUBLISHER'S NOTE

This novel is a work of fiction. Names, characters, places, and incidents either are the product of the author's imagination or are used fictitiously, and any resemblance to actual persons, living or dead, events, or locales is entirely coincidental.

NAL BOOKS ARE AVAILABLE AT QUANTITY DISCOUNTS WHEN USED TO PROMOTE PRODUCTS OR SERVICES. FOR INFORMATION PLEASE WRITE TO PREMIUM MARKETING DIVISION, NEW AMERICAN LIBRARY, 1633 BROADWAY, NEW YORK, NEW YORK 10019.

The first chapter of this book appeared in *Cheyenne Moon*, the fifteenth volume of this series.

SIGNET TRADEMARK REG. U.S. PAT. OFF. AND FOREIGN COUNTRIES
REGISTERED TRADEMARK—MARCA REGISTRADA
HECHO EN CHICAGO, U.S.A.

SIGNET, SIGNET CLASSIC, MENTOR, PLUME, MERIDIAN AND NAL BOOKS are published by New American Library,
1633 Broadway, New York, New York 10019

First Printing, October, 1984

1 2 3 4 5 6 7 8 9

PRINTED IN THE UNITED STATES OF AMERICA

RUFF JUSTICE

He knew the West better than any man alive—a hostile, savage land rife with both violent outlaws and courageous adventurers. But Ruff Justice had a sixth sense that kept him breathing and saw his enemies dead. A scout for the U.S. Cavalry, he was paid to protect the public, and nobody was faster at sniffing out a killer, a crook, a con man—red or white, at close range or far. Anyone on the wrong side of the law would have to reckon with the menace of Ruff's murderously sharp stag-handled bowie knife, with his Colt pistol, and the Spencer rifle he cradled in his arms.

Ruff Justice, gentleman and frontier philosopher—good men respected him, bad men feared him, and women, good and bad, wanted him with all the wildness of the Old West.

1

The door swung open and the fury of the Rocky Mountains blizzard swept into the dark, damp room. The tall man's silhouette filled the doorway briefly and then he staggered in, the door banging shut behind him.

There were six men in the store, which doubled as a saloon in this tiny Colorado mountain town. Almost in unison their heads had turned to the newcomer, their eyes measuring him.

It was apparent immediately that something was wrong. No one in his right mind would be out and about in this weather, not without a compelling reason.

"Are you all right?" Ned Stokes asked. He was the proprietor of the sod-roofed, smoky store. Even inside, Stokes wore his big buffalo coat. The heat from the iron stove in the corner never reached him behind the counter where he worked selling his home-cooked liquor.

"I said, are you all right?"

The tall man stumbled across the room, moving toward the stove, which glowed a dull cherry red. Ice fell from his feet and melted against the floor. His eyebrows and hair were whitened with frost; now that false coloration fell away and they saw that his hair was raven black, worn long.

"Ned!"

That was Andy Buehler. He had risen from the rough bench where he had been sitting sipping whiskey for two days. Now Andy's gaunt face was excited, worried. He pointed at the stained floor and Ned Stokes saw it too.

The stains the tall man was trailing behind him weren't all from snow melt. Some of it was blood.

Ned was out from behind the counter, crossing the room to where the stranger stood weaving before the stove. At the sound of Stokes' approaching footsteps he turned his head, and icy-blue eyes, suddenly alert and wary, were turned on the storekeeper. Eyes that measured and then dismissed the man.

"You hurt, mister?"

"Yes. Let me sit down."

"Sure," Stokes said, "go ahead."

The stranger smiled weakly. "Would you help me?"

"Help you? Sure, all right." Stokes took the arm of the newcomer and helped him down onto the puncheon bench that ran beneath the frosted window beside the stove.

A puddle of liquid had developed beneath the tall man. Water and blood, mingling and trickling away down the crack between the two dark planks at his feet.

"You'd better have someone look at that wound."

"There's really not much point in it. Thank you anyway."

"What is it, gunshot?"

"Yes. Gunshot." Then a savage grimace twisted the stranger's face. Pain clawed at him and shook him violently. Then that, too, passed and he sat there pale and deathly.

"Go get María," he heard Stokes say. That was kind of the man. He felt sorry for María, whoever she was. The wound was not the kind that is pleasant to look at. It was a gut wound—the bad one was—and it had just torn him open.

Stokes was shaking his shoulder and he heard him asking, "Do you want a drink, mister? It'll help some."

He laughed, although it hurt to laugh. "No," he answered. "You see, I don't drink."

He laughed again, but the pain snapped it off. He saw Stokes hovering over him, saw beyond the storekeeper other faces, all unfamiliar. He heard the sound of a woman's voice somewhere, while beside him the stove in its sandbox softly glowed; its warmth barely touched him, which was funny, too, considering how far he had come just to sit beside a fire one last time before that abominable, eternal cold took him down.

She had been there at the hearth when he came back in from the bitter cold outside carrying an armload of firewood. He had seen her silhouette against the weaving red-and-gold flames, seen her turn to him.

"What a surprise! It's a long way to be coming in this weather."

"It was worth it. You make it worth it," she said.

"Let me put this wood down, and I'll make it worth it."

"There's no need, really," she had said. Her face was in shadow, but she seemed to be smiling. He was certain she was smiling.

"Is everything all right?"

"Yes, of course." Her voice was bright, but there was something wrong.

"I guess you'll be staying for supper now. It looks like it's fixing to blow again out there."

She said almost regretfully, "I won't be able to stay. There's just too much to do."

And then she lifted the gun from the folds of her skirt, the big Colt Walker pistol that must have weighed like an anvil in her hand. She two-handed it up, and the muzzle's eye, that big black horrible eye, settled on his gut. He dropped the load of firewood and took half a step backward, and the big Colt thundered. He thought he screamed out her name, but he wasn't sure of that. If he had, the report of the handgun in those close quarters had drowned it out.

The bullet had tagged him hard. He knew right away that it was all over. Pain flooded his guts, like a terrible fire burning away his flesh. He staggered toward the girl, but she made no move to fire again. She just stood there, as cold as the frozen woods outside, watching him.

The cabin door opened before the wind and the man with the rifle came in.

"Damn you," he said to the girl. "I told you to wait."

The injured man had ripped his long coat open and now he managed to claw his pistol out of his holster.

"Watch out!" the girl screamed, and the man in the doorway withdrew quickly as the Colt fired twice, splintering the frame of the cabin door.

One of them appeared at the window. The glass, that precious glass shipped from Denver, was broken out of the frame by the butt of a rifle, and the guns spoke again. The injured man was doubled up with pain, holding his guts together with one hand, but he managed to put one cleanly into the badman's skull and he was blown away from the window.

"Roland!" The girl screamed the injured man's name. He had turned toward her, the Colt held low. He could feel the blood trickling past his waistband, down his thigh. He could barely see her for the pain that surged and then withdrew, surged again, stronger each time.

"Roland, don't shoot me."

She dropped the gun and stepped back toward the fire. He could only look at her wistfully, wondering. There was a catch in her voice and, he thought, tears in her eyes. He couldn't shoot her, he couldn't do her any harm.

"Why . . . ?"

She didn't answer. It was as if she couldn't answer. She stood there, young and beautiful, her fingers to her mouth, and at her feet was the ancient Walker Colt, still warm from the heat of the bullet.

"Why?" He advanced a step and stopped again, wavering. His face was contorted with pain and emotion. She just shook her head.

Her eyes grew suddenly wide and Roland turned quickly, firing as the rifleman in the doorway cut loose again. Roland missed wide. The rifle bullet struck hearthstone and plowed through the fire, kicking up ash and smoldering charcoal.

She screamed, and Roland thought the girl had been hit, but one glance told him that she hadn't. He wanted to take her and twist her head off, to slap her back against the wall, to take her in his arms, to do a thousand wonderful and terrible things to her.

He did nothing like that. He looked at her again, taking in her beauty, wondering at her treachery, and then he backed toward the window, his eyes on the doorway opposite.

In another moment he had stepped up and over the sill. The dead man lay in the snow, his dark, staring eyes gazing skyward. Roland ignored him. He started running, running toward the forest beyond, and the bullets from the cabin followed him.

He had hoped to find his horses in the sheltered cleft that nature had cut into the high, stony bluffs, but they had planned ahead. His horses had been driven off, and without them there just wasn't a chance.

"Walk out," he muttered. He looked skyward. The snow-laden clouds were coming in again, in heavy legions that darkened the skies, shadowed the land, and set the trees to trembling in anticipation.

Walk out—he could have made it another time, although the snow was deep and it was fifteen miles to the nearest community, Stokes' store and the nameless cluster of shacks that had gathered around it.

But not now. Not with the pain gnawing at his belly, not with the deeper pain of betrayal.

"Suck it up, Roland! Move or die." He looked downslope again, shook his head, and started up over the ridge, still holding his stomach, leaving a trail of blood against the new snow.

He was knee-deep in snow much of the way despite his attempts to keep to high ground, to the stony ridges where the wind whipped the snow away. He had packed snow against the fire of his wound, but it hadn't done any good. It was eating him alive with searing pain.

He was halfway to his objective, the Stokes store, before he realized that he had been hit in the shoulder as well. There was a stiffness there that puzzled him until he pulled down the shoulder of his coat and saw the jagged bullet wound. The pain of it was nothing compared to the boring ache in his stomach.

"No chance, my man," Roland said to himself. "You're playing a losing hand."

The storm rolled in, and the wind, blustering and howling, slapped at the wounded man, throwing handfuls of snow at his face. It stung like buckshot and Roland lowered his eyes, bowing his head. The snow was deep, the wind bitterly cold.

He wanted only one thing, warmth. To be warm for one more minute, to feel a fire glowing against his cheek, to not feel the terrible cold that chilled the marrow of his bones and made his muscles hard and brittle.

"If I can make it to the store," he muttered. His voice was lost in the shriek and howl of the wind as he trudged down the long mountain slope through the heavy ranks of pines.

It was hours, it was years, eternity, before he spotted the thin, rising finger of smoke against the briefly clearing sky. Before he spotted the dirty cluster of ramshackle buildings low in the valley.

He stood there for a long while, gazing in disbelief at the tiny town. Then he started forward, thinking of one thing, of the iron stove in Stokes' store, of warmth, of a moment's peace. . . .

"Well?" Stokes demanded.

"I can do nothing," María said. "It is very bad, very bad wound."

"Yeah, all right. I can see that. Thanks, María. Better pull his shirt down again, okay?"

The stout Mexican woman did so. She glanced at the tall man again and crossed herself.

"Anybody know who this jasper is?" Stokes asked. "I swear I've seen him before, but I can't recollect a name."

"I know him," Handy Cross said. The big man continued to sip at his whiskey. "He had a place up over the hogback."

"Miner, was he?"

"No. No, I don't rightly recall what he was doing. Had him a few horses, I recollect." Handy shrugged.

"Any family up there?"

"No. He was all alone, as I recall."

"He had a brother somewhere," Jake Poole put in. "He was in the army, I believe. Something like that."

"Well." Stokes bent over the wounded man and rested his thumb on the big artery in his throat. Then he lifted an eyelid and shook his head. "Anyone who knows where his next of kin might be had best write. This man's dead."

"He was dead when he walked in the door. Beats me how he lasted."

"Yeah." Stokes sighed. "We'll take him out to the woodshed. When we get a thaw, we'll bury him. What did you say his name was, Handy?"

"Justice. That's the name that'll go on his marker. Roland Justice."

"All right. Let's take him out back. Handy, you can write, can't you? Why don't you start on that letter."

"Where's it going? Hell, no one knows rightly where the man's brother might be. If he does get it, why, it'll be too late to do anything about it, won't it? Not much point in writing."

"No, but it's the proper thing to do. Write it. The army will find his brother sooner or later, if he is an army man. At least we'll have done the right thing."

"All right." Handy shrugged. "For all the good it'll do."

He had taken the ink bottle, paper, and pen and seated himself at the far end of the counter to laboriously scratch out the message to the man's next of kin. Handy was right—likely the letter would never reach its intended recipient. If it did, why, it would be months from now, nearly too late to even mourn. Still, you did what was right.

Stokes and Jake Poole carried the body out of the store. They crossed the snow-covered yard and placed the dead man on the floor of the woodshed. Stokes stood looking at the body for a minute and then they went out, leaving Roland Justice to sleep his long sleep.

2

Helen wasn't sure how they had ended up across the room from the rumpled bed, but she didn't mind. Not at all. It was fine. It was wonderful and necessary.

Her back was to the wall. Her legs were lifted and thrown around the waist of the tall, long-haired man, who was standing, holding her in her position. His lips were at her breasts and she was breathing raggedly as he pressed her harder against the wall, driving his length into her with short, powerful movements that turned on little lights in her blond head.

She began to tremble, her fingernails digging into his back; she said something that made no sense at all, and he responded by thrusting against her still harder. Helen's head lolled back; her thighs tightened their grip on his waist. Her eyes were half-open and she could see the intent, somehow vaguely amused look on the mustached man's face.

Then for a moment she could see nothing that was of this world. The colors and swirling mists, the brilliant probing fingers of pleasure clawed at her breasts, her thighs, her womb; her breathing became quick and cadenced. She felt the tall man's hands slip beneath her buttocks and lift her higher, and he leaned forward, his body in constant, maddening motion until the colors and mists collided and there was a brief, fantastic explosion like a shower of meteorites that slowly died away, sparking gold against the blackness of the dizzy faint that lay just a gasp away.

"All right?" he asked, and then he kissed her so that she could only make a muffled answer.

"Yes."

She was breathing hard still, her heart hurling itself against her rib cage. He still had her against the wall and he began to move against her again while Helen thought, God, no, I can't take any more, and simultaneously, Please, please.

She had only had sex with one other man in her life—that had been back home in Ohio with the boy from the farm adjoining theirs. It had been quick, clumsy, heavy with guilt and fear.

And then she had gone to teachers' college, devoted herself to scholastics, and come west to teach where there was a real need.

"Any luck there?" the man with the mustache asked her, and his whisper was thrilling. "Everything all right?"

She just clung to him more tightly. "I'm sorry that I . . . I didn't tell you that last night. I must have humiliated you."

"Not much."

"To criticize your poetry in public like that—it was horrible of me. Snobbish."

"Yes." He kissed her breasts. His strong hands lifted her higher again and she sighed deeply.

"How can you ever forgive me."

He leaned back and smiled. "Just don't do it anymore."

"No, I swear I won't," she said quite seriously, and Ruff Justice threw back his head and laughed in that rich baritone voice of his.

The schoolteacher hadn't done much laughing in her life, apparently. She looked at him, trying to understand, smiling faintly.

Ruff Justice swept back her silky blond hair and kissed her on the throat.

When the stone came flying through the window, it hit him squarely between the shoulder blades.

"Ouch!"

"What happened? Did I . . . ?"

"Nothing you did. Forget it."

He kissed her throat again, feeling her smooth, round breasts flatten against his hard-muscled chest until fresh excitement surged through his loins.

The second rock hit his skull. He stopped, turned, and swallowed a curse.

"What happened?" Helen still clung to him, still had her legs around his waist, her arms around his neck. She was kissing him abstractedly, neck, forehead, cheek, and jaw.

Ruff turned with her and walked across the teacher's bedroom floor to the window where lacy white curtains fluttered in the light breeze. He looked out the window and saw the kid in the torn hat and oversized pants searching the ground for another rock.

"Toss one more and I'll be down to beat you."

"Mister Justice?" the kid asked, his changing voice fluctuating between highs and lows.

"That's right." Helen kissed his neck and reached down to touch his shaft where he entered her, feeling the throbbing of it, the readiness. The scene was hidden by the window frame.

"There's a message come for you out at the fort. The colonel give me a quarter to find you. Important, I guess."

"All right."

Ruff turned away from the window. The kid was still standing, gawking at what he could see of Helen held in Ruff's arms.

"One of my students," Helen said vaguely, and she kissed him again, her tongue grazing the tip of Ruff's tongue, her mouth warm and sweet-tasting. Her body was still lilac-scented, fresh from the morning bath; Ruff had washed her back and they had played house before Justice took her to the bed and got serious about things.

"I've got to go," Ruff said. He placed her on the bed and rolled down beside her, wiping away a lock of hair to look into her gray eyes.

She shook her head. In between her eyebrows two little sulky creases had formed. "No, don't go. It's nothing."

"It might be, Helen. I'd do anything not to go, but it might be very important."

He was thinking of a lesson he had been taught in another sort of school. Of Lieutenant George A. Short, who had been too busy to return to the fort and take his patrol out after a call for help. They had finally reached the old Olmstead place just as the last of the children died beneath a Sioux knife.

There are times when duty just has to supersede personal pleasure. Ruff kissed Helen again and rose. She lay slack and sated on the bed.

"If it's not important . . ." she began.

"Then I'll be back as fast as that old blue roan can run."

"You promise?"

"Yes, I do promise, Helen."

She scooted up on the bed, watching him dress, liking the quick movements of his lean body. She could see the cords of muscle working beneath his pale shoulders, see the deftness of the man, the animal sureness.

Justice was tall, lean, and strong. His dark hair waved gently and dropped past his shoulders. He was brushing it now, using Helen's brush. Then he smoothed his mustache a little. That was very long, too, dropping to his jawline. He was dressed in fringed buckskins with handsome beadwork on the shirt, done by Indian hands, Helen knew. When she had asked about the woman who had done it, Ruff Justice was oddly silent.

He tugged on his boots, which were also fringed. Inside one of the boots was a narrow, extremely sharp skinning knife. Hanging from the back of the gunbelt he now buckled on was a stag-handled bowie. The weight of a big blue Colt revolver counterbalanced the knife's heaviness.

He had a new white stetson that he placed carefully on his head. Jutting from the hatband was a red-tailed hawk's feather. He knotted a long white scarf around his throat loosely, and then he was done, ready to travel. Helen felt a pang of anxiety. "You will be back . . . after. I've never had an experience like this and I'd hate to think it was all over forever."

"I'll be back," Ruff Justice said. It would have been a mistake for him to cross the room and kiss her, and so he just winked, picked up the .56 Spencer repeating rifle that stood in the corner, and went out, leaving the blond and beautiful teacher sprawled on the bed, watching after him.

It had, he thought with some anger, damned well better be an important message.

He rode back toward Fort Lincoln at a canter. The roan liked the pace and the cool, bright day. It moved easily under Ruff Justice. The Missouri River was gleaming in the sunlight, silver-blue, the willows and cottonwoods crowding the banks. Downriver a steamboat tooted twice.

Justice tried to write a bit of doggerel for Helen. Doggerel—that was what she had called it last night when, with schoolmarm pique and eyes flashing, she'd descended on Justice and the knot of boys who'd gathered around to hear a good blood-and-thunder epic. The first cavalry attack had just been gotten through when the woman burst through the schoolboys denouncing the work.

"Of all things to put in these boys' heads! And with all the trouble I have getting just one of them to commit a single line of decent poetry to memory. Like you, Tommy Fann, what are you doing here?"

The boy had hung his head a little. Another kid had come to Ruff's support. "Gee, it's great stuff, Miss Helen. All about the Flint River Massacre last year. Them poems we got at school are all about Greeks and such, and nobody ever heard of them battles."

It was a bad way to characterize the *Odyssey* to a schoolteacher. Helen had flinched and then gone stiff. She had lifted a scolding finger when another kid spoke up.

"Gee, Miss Helen. Everybody knows Ruff Justice is famous for his poems."

"I doubt very much—"

"There's even stuff about him in eastern papers. I got a clipping right here," the boy had said, and then Dan Schorr of the *Philadelphia Inquirer* came to Ruff's rescue. Justice always had wondered about that review, but it may have had something to do with the fact that Justice had stood drinks for the man all night long.

" 'An American triumph,' " Miss Helen read from the folded, yellowed newspaper clipping, " 'with the Buffalo Bill Cody Show that has come to visit our fair city is the famous 'poet scout,' Mister Ruffin T. Justice. Mr. Justice favored us all with a reading of his rugged, bright and unique poetry. . . .' "

At about that point, if Ruff recalled, Schorr had fallen off his chair, but he had heard at least a few lines, and he'd needed something to fill his column up the next day. He went on with a lot of stuff about bucolic Homers and Western individualism, unique metrical structures, and all. It meant nothing; what criticism does? But Miss Helen was impressed, and in the end she had invited Ruff to tea.

"Helen . . ." Ruff began again, trying to find a line or two to give to the lady. But her name was a barrier. Felon? he thought, and he shook his head. Melon? He threw the whole idea out. She would have to get along without her own poem.

Sergeant Mack Pierce was at his desk in the orderly room when Ruff Justice walked in. The big first shirt looked up smiling, but the smile faded as he saw Justice.

"Hello, Ruffin."

"Hello, Mack. A kid in town said there was something going on."

"That's right. The colonel wanted to talk to you," the NCO said, lifting his massive bulk from his tortured chair. "I'll see if he's available now."

Mack was being awfully formal, Justice thought, frowning. What was it, another complaint to the army about their rather flamboyant civilian scout? He hoped not. MacEnroe always went on too long with his lectures, and he hated it when Ruff yawned at him.

Pierce was back. "Go on in, Ruffin."

Ruff looked at Mack, seeing some sort of trouble in his eyes, not quite reading what it was. He shrugged and passed by into the colonel's office.

Fort Abraham Lincoln's commanding officer was standing before his map, staring blankly at it, his hands clasped behind his back. He turned slowly to face Ruff. "Hello, Ruffin. Have a seat."

"All right." Justice sat in the corner, balanced his hat on his knee, and waited for the colonel to speak.

MacEnroe didn't waste time. "It's your brother, Ruff. He's dead." The colonel saw Justice's eyes go stony and cold. He muttered, "I'm sorry," and handed the letter to Justice. It was from someone named Handy Cross out in Colorado.

To the United States Army,

 This letter is bound for a man called Ruffin
Justice, who is in the army. It is to tell him that his
brother, who is named Roland Justice, is dead.
Sorry. He was all shot up, and though we tried to
help him, he just died anyways.

Handy Cross
at the Stokes' Store
Hardship, Colorado

Ruff read the letter twice and then handed it back
to Colonel MacEnroe. He wasn't stunned; after all,
life was hard out there and people just kept on
dying—hard weather, Indians, wild creatures. There
were hundreds of ways to die. Yet Roland hadn't
died that way, had he?

"He was all shot up . . ."

"I'm sorry, Ruff," the colonel said again. "I really
didn't even know you had a brother."

Ruff smiled slightly. "We always kind of thought it
was best for the world if we stayed as far away from
each other as possible. Two of us together was a little
too much for comfort." Ruff lifted his eyes. "I'll be
wanting some leave."

"I knew you would."

"Sorry, Colonel, but I've got to go over there and
see what happened."

"We'll get along." MacEnroe was unusually pliant.
Damn the man—he actually did have a heart.

"Thanks." Ruff stood, put his hat on again, nodded,
and went out the door. Mack Pierce had Ruff's back
pay ready in cash in case the scout needed it. Ruff
scooped up the gold, said a hasty good-bye to Pierce,
and went out.

Standing for a moment on the plankwalk outside
the orderly room, Justice looked up at the crystal-
blue skies. A squad of soldiers was drilling across the

parade ground, Sergeant Ray Hardistein's distinctive voice calling out orders. Smoke rose from the cookhouse. Justice was far away in thought, recalling the lean older brother he had looked up to and then regarded as a rival. They had wrestled for fun, fought quite seriously with knuckles and stones, been rivals for the same girl, been separated by the fortunes of battle, fate . . .

And he was dead.

The sutler's store was almost directly across from the orderly room and Ruff Justice walked that way, leading the lazy-appearing blue roan. He loosely hitched the horse and went inside. Harry Grange was the new sutler and he nodded, smiling pleasantly.

"Anything today, Mister Justice?"

"Just about everything that a single horse can carry. I'm going on a long trip, Harry."

"Sioux?"

"No. Coyotes."

Harry added up the bill. The sacks of salt, coffee, and flour, the bag of dried fruit, the boxes of ammunition, sat on the counter. For the rest of it, Ruff would have to live off game. He wasn't going to kill the horse for his own comfort. It was a hell of a long ride, but he was going.

"He was all shot up, and though we tried to help him, he just died anyways."

Ray Hardistein came into the sutler's store before Ruff had gotten out. The sergeant spotted his friend and said, "Say, Ruffin, some of the boys were wondering—"

"Hello, Ray," Justice said, cutting Hardistein off. Then, with his arms full of his purchases, Ruff was out the door, loading his saddlebags.

"What do you suppose is the matter with the scout?" Harry Grange asked.

"I don't know." Ray Hardistein shook his head

and watched Justice for a time through the greenish window of the sutler's store. "But I've seen that look before, Harry. And I'll tell you this—be glad you're here and not at the end of that man's trail."

3

The Colorado Rockies began to bulk large against the skyline. Great purple sprawling things, they cast their miles-long shadows across the green velvet foothills. There was snow on the peaks, snow in the gashes on the flanks of the mammoth mountains where the sun never reached. Late sunlight glinted off a field of ice on the northern face of a pyramid-shaped mountain. The wind was cold at the lone rider's back. The land ahead was awesome, seemingly untamable.

The blue roan was trail-weary, gaunted. Ruff Justice was ready to swing down and camp, but he rode on. The lone trapper he had met at Bent Creek had told him of a tiny settlement on this side of the mountains where a man could find food, a bed, grain for his horse. It was the last of these that interested Ruff the most, although he had no objections to food and a bed.

The nights had been cold. When the wind blew from the west, there was the taste of ice, of menace to it. He glanced again to the high mountains where the late sun made purple shadows, dull blue monuments. A notch in a high peak showed the red gold of the dying sun brilliantly.

"Where in the hell is the place?" Ruff asked irritably. The roan simply plodded on.

The town, settlement, collection of shacks—whatever you wanted to call it—should have been near here, at the base of the foothills where the Charles Creek ran down out of the high country. It wasn't. Since dawn Ruff had been expecting to see it sprout up out of the hills. Either he or the trapper had a poor idea of distances.

It was fairly obvious that he wasn't going to make it that night, and he grumbled another curse. He patted the roan's neck and started looking around for a place to camp, preferably on the high ground. His journey had been free of Indian trouble, but the trapper had told him that the mountain Utes were fussing some. They'd burned out a rancher or two, scalped a pair of greenhorns, slaughtered stock where they could. The army wasn't having any luck, and Ruff could see why. It would take a different kind of force than the United States cavalry wielded to root Indians out of these hills.

He saw a small hill that was virtually barren but for a handful of oaks at its crown. There was grass there as well, some chaparral off to the south. It looked like a fire had cleared most of the hill at one time and left a little thatching up top. The site suited Ruff Justice and he rode that way, the roan almost groaning with the thought of climbing a hill.

What the horse needed was a good week's rest, plenty of grain and care. Much as Justice hated the idea, he was beginning to think he was going to have to switch off horses before he made Ned Stokes' store up on the other side of the mountains. What was it they called their little town, Hardship? Ruff looked at the rapidly darkening mountains, feeling again the breath of constant winter. Yes, he thought, that name likely fits the place.

It had to be a hardship just to exist from year to year in these mountains. Yet Roland must have liked it. Why else would his brother have settled in here? There was a raw, primitive beauty to the mountains. No, it was more than that; ask anyone who has seen the Rockies up close. There is a grandeur, a vast timelessness that overshadows an individual life with its frailty and tiny span. It engulfs a man, somehow makes him larger by simply existing. It makes a man feel very small, and by some stroke of magic consequently fills him up with the stuff of life, makes him pleased with the idea of his own being, his ability to stand on two legs and appreciate the beauty, the primitive order around him.

"Still doesn't explain why anyone'd want to live here," Ruff grumbled. He swung down stiffly. "It's cold, isolated, and lonely."

Not that Justice hadn't spent time in all of those conditions, but when he wanted to see a light, he wanted it. He wanted a woman around, one in evening gowns or dance-hall glitter. He wanted a meal served on china from time to time. True, he needed to come into the wilderness, craved it, but his other side wouldn't let him dwell in it. He wasn't cut out to be a hermit.

"Not unless I was well equipped with hermettes."

The roan didn't appreciate that one. It was tired, needed a good rubbing—which it got—and oats and corn—which it didn't. Ruff ate biscuits and smoked meat from an antelope he had taken three days before. He was getting to where he hated antelope meat. He hoped to God he found that settlement, come morning.

It trotted right into the camp and sat down facing Ruff Justice, who hadn't even had time to grab for his gun. It sat there, big and slavering, picket-sided, yellow-eyed, its massive head weaving erratically, its shaggy coat fitting it loosely.

"Where in hell did you come from?" Justice asked. He slowly drew his Colt while he looked at the big wolf or dog or whatever the hell it was. It had feet that would make elephant tracks, a jaw that looked like it could crack granite boulders to look for the marrow.

"Hungry?" Ruff tossed the whole of the remaining haunch of antelope to the dog, and it fell on it savagely, grumbling and growling. It's eyes flashed as it looked to Ruff, making sure he wasn't going to try to take it back.

There was no worry on that score. A man would have to be crazy to try to take something from that dog's mouth. Ruff scooted back, not entirely comfortable with this beast, which looked as if it might just have trouble remembering where the antelope haunch left off and Ruff's leg began.

He didn't want the thing around, but there wasn't a good way to get rid of it. It snorted and growled and tore at the meat, stripping the bone that it held between its massive paws. Lost from a wagon train? Or was it a half-breed wolf?

There wasn't going to be much sleep that night with the dog close by. In the morning he could easily leave it behind. It would have to fend for itself or die. Maybe that was cruel, but it is that way with every creature on the earth.

Ruff didn't like having dogs with him. Not that he disliked them, but they were a liability in his line of work. They tended to bark, for one thing, and to make noise at the wrong time on the plains was to die.

There had been little Dooley Dog once, a long while back, small, tough, voiceless. The two of them had tolerated each other for a time, and then the dark-eyed woman had taken it away. . . . All a long time ago.

The wolf-dog just lay there gnawing on the bone, its stomach growling still, its throat making pleasured sounds.

"Now you can get on out of here," Ruff said. The dog lifted its head. The yellow eyes shone in the faint light. He could smell its coat. There was another smell, that of a festering wound, and Justice cursed himself as he rose to walk near the dog.

"Easy now," he said softly.

The dog rumbled deep in its throat and withdrew a little, coiling, its hackles rising. Ruff stretched out a hand and the dog, its glassy yellow eyes still gleaming, came forward quickly, snapping at it with long white teeth.

"Take it easy, big boy," Ruff said. Justice, he told himself, you're a damned fool if you stick your hand out there again. You'll nevermore play the fiddle. But then he never had. He stuck out his hand slowly, a fraction of an inch at a time, and all the while the wolf dog was growling, braced and watchful.

Ruff let his hand dangle inches from the dog's muzzle and it sniffed at it, something working deep within its animal brain, some fear colliding with need and trust and want. A gigantic pink tongue lolled out and was wiped across Justice's fingers. Ruff exhaled slowly and patted the big dog's neck. It groaned and flopped on its side, emaciated flanks heaving. Ruff found the arrow behind the shoulder blade, high up.

"Got you, didn't they?" He could just feel the shaft of the arrow. The dog had broken it off so that there was only an inch or so above the hide. Beneath the hide was a festering wound, a knot of infection the size of Ruff's fist.

Justice sat back on his haunches, watching the dog. "You have brought me a problem, dog, you know that?" The dog's eyes flickered slightly. "Yes, you have. You're a goner if that arrowhead doesn't come out."

But there was only one way to get it out, and that was to take a knife and cut into the creature's shoulder. They weren't quite intimate enough for Justice to feel any confidence at all about that sort of operation.

"Sorry, old man," Justice said, and the dog continued to stare at him, the yellow eyes savage yet
hopeful—or was that imagination? Men see a lot of
traits in animals that just aren't there, Ruff thought.
There was a lady in Bismarck who had seen a squirrel die and seen another run to it, and she had built
up a story of the mate mourning for the squirrel that
had died. She knew that was what was happening by
the way it came and attended to the other. She
hadn't noticed that every time the squirrel came to
where the dead one lay, it took a little bite of flesh
and ran away to devour it.

Nowadays there were lots of scientists and teachers
from the East coming out to see the noble redman
who despised them, the noble animals that were in-
different to them. They knew that cougars were
maligned and proud, free and noble—they'd never
seen a herd of spring lambs a lion has prowled
through, killing for the hell of it. The truth was
there was no nobility in the animal, but a need to
find nobility in the minds of men.

None of that had much to do with Ruff's predica-
ment. There was an animal suffering here. If he
helped it, or tried to, he would probably end up
having to kill it. That was the irony of it. The dog
would be hurt by the knife. It wouldn't understand
the hurt, and it would strike out.

"What do I do, old man?" Ruff asked. He put a
hand out slowly and stroked the massive head of the
huge dog, rubbing its ear with his thumb. He knew
what the answer should have been—he should have
just drawn his bowie and put an end to the whole
business by severing the dog's jugular.

"No." Ruff wasn't made that way. "I'm going to
have at it, big fellow. I hope to God you understand
that I'm helping you."

He built a tiny fire and held the blade of the
skinning knife over it. The dog's eyes glittered in the

firelight. Ruff Justice stroked the dog's shoulder. Then he moved in close, hunched over the animal, which lay still, breathing very rapidly, its eye watching.

Justice took a slow breath. The skinning knife touched flesh and sank into the hide. The dog stiffened and it whined pitiably. The knife slashed deeper into the wound. A putrid smell rose from it as the steel blade lanced the pocket of pus. The dog began to writhe, its hind legs moving in a running motion, but it remained on its side, it gleaming yellow eyes on Ruff Justice, who continued to dig for the arrowhead that had caused this. When he found it, he pulled it free.

Ruff sagged back on his haunches and looked at the broken shaft of the Ute arrow, at the obsidian head, serrated, almost artistically chipped. Ruff cast it away and patted the dog's side. He had a small bottle of carbolic in his saddlebags, and he went and got it, pouring it on the wound. If the dog hadn't bitten him yet, he wouldn't over the sting of the carbolic acid.

He hoped.

The dog quivered again and then lay still. Ruff corked the bottle of carbolic and went back to his bed. He dragged it farther upslope beneath the big oaks. He still intended to try to sleep that night. He had done what he could for the dog; now let it live or die as nature intended.

Ruff rolled up into the blankets and watched the distant stars for a long while before sleep closed his eyes.

He woke at dawn and he was first aware of the smell, of the closeness of a body. He opened an eye and saw the great shaggy beast lying next to him. And there was a yellow eye, like a topaz in the sunlight, looking at him.

"Damn you, you're a quiet thing, aren't you?" Ruff said. He rolled out of his bed and sat rubbing his head. The dog, sitting up itself, watched.

"Get away! Think I've adopted you, you great ugly brute?" The dog cocked its head to one side appraisingly. "How's that wound?" Justice asked.

He moved nearer, stroking the dog's neck. He could see only that the knot had gone down, that the dog seemed to have no fever. Its nose was cool, eyes bright.

"You're just waiting for breakfast, are you?"

Well, it was welcome to breakfast, and then Justice would be moving on and the dog would be left behind. There was no way it was going to keep up with the roan in his condition. "Sorry. You need a nurse, and I've got other things on my mind."

But the dog would survive. It was tough, rangy, and very large. Its back came to mid-thigh as Ruff stood and stretched and the dog rose with him, expectantly. It had a head like a grizzly's, and an appetite like one. Ruff had coffee, three biscuits, three or four ounces of antelope meat. The dog ate the other haunch.

After breakfast Ruff saddled up, paying no attention at all to the dog, which lay chewing on a bone. He glanced at it once as he swung up and then just turned the roan out of the camp and headed down the long slope.

When he looked back fifteen minutes later, he saw the big dog loping after him. It ran awkwardly with that wounded shoulder, and Justice knew it wouldn't be keeping up for long. He lifted the roan into its customary canter and rode on, the wind across the plains toying with his dark hair, lifting his buckskin fringes.

Half an hour later as he slowed to cross a little creek he looked back again, seeing nothing. The dog had been left far behind. Tough . . . but that was the way things had to be.

At noon he spotted the little town sitting up next to the folded foothills, smoke rising from several iron chimneys. The roan was already tired and Ruff made up his mind to switch off. With that in mind, he looked for a livery barn as he walked the length of the rocky, humped, and rutted street.

There wasn't much to see of the town. Three false-fronted buildings, one of them—the general store—painted barn-red. There were a handful of adobe-brick buildings and then you were out of town. Ruff halted just before that happened.

The livery wasn't marked, but it smelled right, and unless the man kept horses in his parlor, that's what the place was.

Ruff went in, leading the roan. He dropped the reins and looked up and down the stalls at the other horses.

"Help you?" the voice behind him said. Ruff turned to face the red-bearded man in coveralls. "You! Dammit, they said you were dead!"

"Did they?" Ruff asked dryly. "You're thinking of someone else, my friend."

"I am, am I? How there could be two gents that look like you, I can't imagine."

"I need a horse," Ruff went on as if there had been no interruption. "My roan there is kind of worn down, but he's a good one and he's sound. You got anything we could work a bargain on?"

The red-bearded man had eased up nearer and he stood staring at Justice, shaking his head. "When'd you start wearing a mustache?"

"About seventy-four years ago, I'd guess." Ruff was in no mood for the man's questions. "How about that buckskin?"

"That's Ned Travers' horse," the man answered.

"Which ones are yours?" Ruff asked.

The bearded man was nearly eyeball to eyeball with Ruff now. "Let me get this straight. Is your name Justice, or ain't it?"

"Yes, it is. That's right. How about the sorrel there, the one with the blaze face?"

"I thought it was Justice, all right."

"The sorrel?"

"That ain't mine either. Take a look at that other roan."

"No," Ruff said. Even from a distance he could see he didn't want the roan. Age showed, and ring hoof. "I need something a little tougher. I'm going over the mountains."

"To Hardship?"

"That's right."

"You see—I do recall. What kind of joke is this you've been playin' anyway? Say, did you ever find that man you were lookin' for?"

"What man?" Ruff asked, his eyes narrowing.

"You know. The one with the tattoos."

"Tattoos?"

"Yeah. All over his whole body, you said, everywhere but his face."

"No," Ruff said, "I never found him. I didn't say what I wanted him for, did I?"

The hostler tugged at his beard and eyed Ruff as if one of them was crazy. "No, you never did, come to think of it, but don't tell me you don't remember."

"What about the little gray?"

"That's a good piece of horseflesh, mister. Nice little pony, mountain-bred. He'll do the job. 'Course . . . they say the high pass is closed. Snow slide."

"Is that so?" Ruff was looking the horse over, lifting its hooves, running a hand along its flank. "Who said that? Where can I find someone that knows for sure?"

"I don't know. Maybe it was Ed Greenbrier. He had some traplines up high until the Utes ran him out. I think it was maybe Ed who knows for sure. He'll be sleeping in the Happy Times. That's the middle saloon." The hostler scratched his chin, his eyes growing shrewd. "What would you say to a hundred plus your roan for that gray horse?"

"I'd say I'd rather walk," Ruff Justice answered. "I'll give you fifty to boot if you'll let me trade you when I get back from Hardship."

"Well, all right, but I'm taking a beating. Say, wasn't you telling me you had a few horses of your own over there?" the hostler asked.

"Was I?"

"Well, sure." The puzzlement was back on his face. "You said you had yourself a little herd—thirty horses, I think it was—some Morgan blood in there. Matter of fact, you told me you had a pure-blood Morgan.

"Fifty dollars?" Ruff had slipped the gold coins from his boot and now he thumbed them into the man's palm. "Will you shift my saddle and gear for me?"

"Sure, sure I'll do that. You going to the Happy Times?"

"That's right."

"All right. I'll have the kid bring him up. And say," the man asked, looking toward the door, "do you want me to stable *that* up too or just throw a saddle on it?"

"Do what?" Ruff turned toward the door of the stable and looked where the hostler was pointing. There sat the dog, pink tongue dangling, eyes bright.

It lifted its tail and thumped it down once as Ruff approached. He rested a hand briefly on the dog's massive head. "Need a dog?" he asked the hostler.

"What would I feed it? If I turned my back, I'd be afraid of losing horses. No, thanks, Mister Justice."

Ruff went out of the stable then and stood, hat in hand, rubbing his head. He looked up the dusty street, past the town, to the mountains. To the mountains where Roland Justice had been killed. Because of a tattooed man? Or did that mean anything? After this length of time Ruff would be lucky if he ever found out, and he knew it. Still, you tried. That was

all you could do. And if luck was with you, then
there was retribution. You can't wait for the law;
there is no law. Just vengeance. And those high
mountains were as good a place as any for the killing.

4

"No. Hell, no." The man with the yellow mustache and tobacco-colored teeth shook his head and drank the whiskey Ruff Justice had paid for. "You can't get across the mountains right now. Not even as far as Hardship. Things are closed down tight."

"Snow?"

"That's right," Greenbrier said. "Snow and rock and half a forest that slid off when the avalanche hit. I was there, not a mile off, and it sounded like nothing you've ever heard. Ever see an avalanche? God almighty. You'd think the earth was just splitting open, tearing itself apart. I got down out of there—"

"There has to be a way."

"Does there? Why? No, there ain't a way unless a man was to go three hundred miles south, take the Gibson cut-off and ride back. No, hell, no, that wouldn't even work."

"There's the old Ute Trail," someone from a nearby table said.

"Oh, shit, Cranston—you think anyone is going to take that damned trail? Go back to you beer."

Ruff asked, "What was he talking about?"

"Old trail. It ain't bad. Little steep, some broken, likely some snow above eight thousand."

"What's wrong with it?"

"Utes." Greenbrier looked at Ruff as if he were a lunatic. "Utes all over it. They're coming down into the hills for their big medicine war. They've got a good two dozen whites tallied up in the last few months. There were a few sodbusters trying to make it over east. Utes got 'em all. A war chief named Half Moon is the devil that's doin' it all. Yes," Greenbrier paused for another shot of whiskey. "They got the entire Chamliss family—man, wife, two kids."

"Dog," the man at the next table muttered.

"Huh? What's that, Cranston?"

"The man's got the Chamliss's dog."

"That big son of a bitch?" Greenbrier pursed his lips. "Yes, they had a big dog. You got it now?"

Ruff told him, "I found one with an arrow in it. I'd be willing to leave it here with anyone that needs a good big dog."

"That one? Don't trust it. Chamliss was crazy to take it in. Half wolf, if you ask me," Greenbrier said.

"Half bear," Cranston muttered.

"Huh? Shit, Cranston, if you want to be in the conversation move over and introduce yourself to the man."

"Don't have to introduce myself. Justice knows me."

"This ain't that one; it's his brother. Haven't you got eyes? How the hell's a man get so drunk on beer?" Greenbrier poured himself a whiskey.

"What about this Ute Trail? Can you sketch it out for me?" Ruff wanted to know.

"Sketch it out. Sure I can sketch it out, but you don't want to take it, mister. I'm not making up tales. The Utes are everywhere up there, and they're mad. Half Moon wants every white in the mountains dead. That's his idea."

"If you could just sketch it out," Ruff suggested with a smile that made it clear he wasn't just making a request.

"I wouldn't be in a hurry to die, is all," Greenbrier mumbled.

"I appreciate your concern," Justice said, "but it's important. I've got to get over the hump."

"All right," Greenbrier said, shrugging deeply. He got a piece of paper bag from the bartender, borrowed a pencil, and sat down, sketching the country around roughly, little X's marking the peaks. Greenbrier was no artist, but like all men who lived out in rough country, he knew the land, his directions, distances, and relative altitudes. It was a matter of survival. The trapper finished his map with another word or two of advice, which Justice ignored. He was going. His mind was set on that, and there was nothing anyone could say to talk him out of it.

"By the way," Justice asked after Greenbrier was finished, "ever see anything of the tattooed man?"

"No. You know, I was just going to ask you what happened with that business."

"I don't really know."

"Your brother didn't tell you?"

"Haven't seen him for years."

"I seen the tattooed man," Cranston said. He deliberately stared down at the table, not turning his head. Greenbrier had him brownbeaten and sulky.

"Where?" Ruff asked.

"Over at Honey Springs. This was some time back, maybe two months or so."

"What was he doing?"

"Doing? Nothing, when I saw him. Just taking a bath in the springs below town. Had his clothes off, and I just sat for a while staring at the tattoos he has curling all over him. Then he kind of says, 'What are you looking at?' in the tone of voice that means, Go away. So I went away."

"You know his name?"

"No, sir, I surely don't."

"Does he have an accent?"

"Like is he from the South or France or something?" Cranston said. "No, I don't think so."

"And you don't know, either of you, what my brother wanted with him."

"Why, yes, sir, I reckon I know." Cranston lifted his eyes. "He wanted to kill him, was what he wanted."

Ruff Justice rode out in the afternoon. The sun was already dropping toward the dark, bulky mountains. The snowy peaks, thirteen and fourteen thousand feet up, gleamed in the sunlight. The gray moved out briskly toward the old Ute Trail; behind Ruff Justice the big dog loped.

Outside of the town the blue spruce and the pines surrounded the trail, which wound into the foothills. Ruff passed a burnt-out farm two miles out. He didn't know whose it had been, but he stopped for a minute and looked down at the charred timbers, the sad piles of ash in the grassy meadow. The dog threw back his head and howled long and mournfully.

Ruff rode on. The wind off the high peaks was growing cold, and he stopped to pull his buffalo coat on. There were going to be plenty of cold days ahead. It was always winter near the timberline, and if those clouds easing in from the north proved to have more than bluster in them, it would be a hard trail, with or without the Utes.

At dusk he found a small valley where the lodgepole pines broke the prevailing wind and there was graze for the little gray. The horse hardly seemed tired. A little rill ran down out of a tangle of gray, vine-wrapped boulders, and Justice made coffee, risking fire. Farther on he wouldn't be able to light one.

Then, warmed by the coffee, he sat down to watch the land go dark. The pines were spread across the hills in dark, endless ranks, their serrated tips carving silhouettes against the orange-and-purple sky. The valleys below, in pockets, were silver-green, the shadows slowly creeping across them. Beyond the plains was red-brown and pale violet, with here and there a spot of gold where pure, bright sunlight touched the prairie through the notches in the high mountains.

It was all quite beautiful and Ruff Justice could have enjoyed the settling dusk, the wild and savage scenery—if it weren't for the fact that there was someone on his backtrail.

The dog smelled it. From time to time it grumbled a low-voiced warning to the wind. Justice had seen only the horse, small and distant, a tiny dark speck that moved along the trail, winding into the mountains.

They had told Ruff Justice that he was crazy to go into the mountains. What had they told the man who was following him?

"There's trouble coming," Justice said. The dog, its head on its paws, thumped its tail once. That seemed to be the limit of its excitement, as if it was afraid to allow itself too much happiness, knowing that humans continued to go away, to lie down and die.

Ruff waited until it was full dark, marking the spot where he had last seen the horse on the backtrail, estimating its progress since then.

It was likely nothing. Probably just another madman riding into the domain of the savage Utes under Half Moon. Sure. And there would probably be two moons rising that night.

"It's me they want," Justice said. Why, he didn't know. But if someone in this area wanted him dead, the odds were strong that it was because they had known Roland Justice. Known him and been involved in his death.

"At any rate," Justice said, "it's only proper to go down and introduce myself."

He checked his guns against that occasion.

The moon was rising when Justice started down the valley afoot. Maybe he was making too much of this, but then he wasn't going to risk death on carelessness.

He found the man two miles below his camp in a small hollow, rolled up in his blanket. Ruff went in through the trees, his pistol in his hand, his feet whispering across the grass. He had no trouble coming up on the man. He crouched down, the Colt ready, pointed at the man's head.

"All right," Justice said. "Mind a little conversation?"

He didn't mind anything in the world. He was stone dead in his bedroll, his throat slashed from ear to ear. Ruff saw the dark pool beneath the body, saw starlight on the partly open eyes. He stepped back quickly into the shadows of the trees and stood listening.

There was nothing to be heard but the wind whispering in the trees, the distant hooting of an owl. Ruff's eyes combed the darkness, searching.

What the hell is this? he wondered silently. Someone thinking this man was me?

That was possible. Maybe someone riding after Ruff with a message. Concerning his brother? The tattooed man? When he had rolled up to sleep, another hunter had come . . . or the Utes? It could be them as well. They wouldn't have had time to take the scalp.

"Too damned much guessing, not enough knowing," Ruff told himself aloud. The only thing certain was that there was a killing man out there.

Ruff slipped out of the little hollow, working through the trees toward his camp, which was as he had left it, the gray quietly grazing, the dog dozing. No one was around, or the dog would have let Ruff know. No one with any sense would come around that animal anyway.

Ruff rolled up in his blankets, but there was little sleep that night. When dawn gilded the plains, he rolled out and walked to his cold fire, starting it again, thrusting his tiny coffeepot into the licking red flames. The grass beneath his boots was frosted, crunching as he saddled up the gray. He warmed the bit for a moment inside his shirt before slipping it into the horse's mouth.

When he was finished saddling, the coffee had boiled and he poured his tin cup full. He stood sipping it, watching the trail below him, the endless expanse of blue-green forest, the birds arcing across the sky.

He had a notion to go back down and look over the body of the man he had found last night, but decided against it. He wanted to be getting up the trail. Those clouds were still building in the northern skies and he had no wish to be on this side of the mountains if snow fell.

He rode out into the high country with a harsh wind blowing, the dog loping along behind. Ruff gave it no encouragement, but it was apparently going to stick with him. Short of shooting it, there was no way to drive it off. It needed someone, something, as all living things do. Ruff didn't have the heart to take what little it had, himself, away. And if the dog had survived this long, Ruff thought it probably couldn't hurt to have it around.

The clouds formed great gray battlements above the peaks. The trees swayed in unison along the trail, creaking together, bough rubbing bough, with occasionally the loud popping of a branch breaking free. When the wind gusted, pine cones fell in a wooden shower and ice broke from the high boughs to rain down.

Ruff stopped three times in the first two miles to look back down. He saw nothing, but then he hadn't seen the man yesterday. Whoever he was, Indian or white, he was very good. It's not that easy to kill a sleeping man, no matter what some might think. There's an instinct for survival that awakens a man to a threat in the night, a suspected or real threat. Subtle senses that scream out and bring the body's defenses to the surface.

The man with the slashed throat hadn't even moved. A ghost might have done the job.

Ruff looked ahead of him now, seeing the uptilting of the land, the tangled, jagged ranges twisting away to the north and south for hundreds of miles. It wasn't going to be much fun. He patted the gray's neck and headed toward the marker peak that Greenbrier had indicated, a small, crumbling knoll that had been scooped out on one side. It jutted up above the trees, and Ruff, cresting the trail he now rode, saw the old Ute Trail running up along the sides of the high peaks, a thread placed against the mountains, a treacherous narrow path hardly wide enough for a horse, where the slapping wind seemed capable of picking a man off the slope and throwing him down into the incredibly steep canyons like a drifting leaf.

If that wasn't enough, he ran a very good chance of meeting a bloodthirsty party of painted Utes who wouldn't mind in the least using Ruff Justice as a sort of appetizer for their feast of destruction.

And they did like that long silky hair.

Ruff smiled. He took off his white scarf and tied his hat down, knotting the scarf under his chin. Then, lifting the collar of his buffalo coat, he started on, up the Ute trail, toward Hardship, his brother's killers ahead of him, a murderer behind him, and somewhere out there a half-mad Ute war chief and a tattooed man with his secrets, secrets Ruff couldn't even guess at. He knew only one thing about the tattooed man: Roland had wanted to kill him.

A tattooed man made Ruff think of one thing: of the sea, where for centuries men had tattooed marks upon themselves to propitiate the gods of the sea, to keep the violent death the sea was notorious for at bay. There were other reasons for tattoos, other places men and even women were accustomed to them. Certain Indian tribes were famed for the beauty of their tattoos—like the Seminoles. But no one had mentioned that the tattooed man was an Indian.

"And Roland," Ruff Justice told the gray horse above the wail of the wind, "was indeed a sailing man."

He had gone away at the age of eighteen, the year before the Civil War began, to sail on a barkentine out of Charleston. To sail to the Orient—that was all Ruff knew about it, the Orient. He thought that their cargo had been indigo and rice and that they had returned not to Charleston, where Fort Sumter perched precariously like the fuse to a vast powder keg, but to England, supposedly neutral, but actually favoring the Confederacy. That was the last Ruff had seen of his brother. There must have been dozens of other voyages, to ports Ruff had never even heard of, and there had been time to make many an enemy.

He was riding the long trail now, into the Ute mountains. From high up the slopes, from far above the timberline, he heard a deep wailing, like a mournful wolf—but that may have been imagination, a memory of another time on another mountain when the Wind Wolf had called to him. It didn't bother the dog any. The big creature plodded on, its tongue dangling. Wherever the man in buckskins led him, the big dog would follow willingly.

Darkness came early in the mountains and Justice began to look for a camping place shortly after noon. It wouldn't do at all to be caught out on that trail after dark. As he rode higher, he began to encounter pockets of ice alongside the trail, patches of snow, and the wind from the north was strengthening. At eight thousand feet he found snow, as Greenbrier had promised.

The wind now spoke with the shrieking voices of a thousand demons, screaming warnings, threats, imprecations. Ruff camped in a tiny hollow to the side of the trail. There could be no fire on this night, and so he simply sat there, hunched forward, a blanket around his shoulders. The dog was nearby, as was the horse, ice on its back, its head hanging.

That was the night the Utes came.

If he hadn't pulled off the trail early, he would have ridden right into them. It was a small party, six men all mounted, their horses painted for war. Ruff saw his own horse's head go up, heard the soft, nearly thrumming growl of the big dog. He placed his hand on the dog's neck and it fell silent. Listening, Ruff heard them then. He heard a hoof strike stone, heard a man complain, a horse blow, and he slowly unsheathed his big Spencer repeater.

Darkness was nearly upon them and a light, wind-driven rain had begun to fall. The dog stirred, not liking the smell of the Utes, but Ruff stilled it again, hoping to God the thing would stay quiet, because if it spoke, he would die. The Utes would die, too—some of them—but Ruff wouldn't have a chance, caught in that tiny hollow.

"Let us camp now . . ." He heard the wind-twisted words clearly. It was a tongue he knew, taught to him by the woman Yarna in other times when Ruff had been with the Utes. Not these, but a northern people who had wished for peace and been unable to find it.

"So cold for us. The horses are weary."

"But Half Moon will want . . ."

The rest of the words were yanked away from Ruff's ears by the swirling wind, but he knew now all he needed to know. These were a part of Half Moon's renegade band, warring men, and they wanted a place to camp out of the wind. And Ruff Justice had their shelter.

"Look here," he heard a Ute say. "The small hollow. Let us camp there. Small Hands is right, it will soon snow."

Justice sank back against the side of the hollow. There was no way out. He had the big .56 Spencer in his hands. He could see the silhouettes of the

Indians now, see their impatiently stamping horses, the steam rising from their nostrils.

It was cold, very cold. The next words Ruff heard chilled him to the marrow.

"There," another Ute said, "a white."

Ruff's thumb hooked the hammer of his rifle. A few of them would go down with him anyway. But the Utes weren't coming toward him at all now. They had silently mounted their ponies and they were starting down the mountainside again. Justice hastily saddled, his teeth chattering with the cold, his fingers numb, his heart racing.

And then he heard the scream, and he knew it was too late to help the man, whoever he was. The Utes had him. After a while the screams died away and the silence of the night descended.

Ruff led the gray out of the hollow, mounted, and started up the trail away from the little band of Utes. It was a tough way to go, the way the man down the trail had died. But then he hadn't shown much mercy when he had slit the throat of the sleeping cowboy.

That was who it had to be, of course. The killer who was trailing Ruff Justice. No one else was out and about, not along the Ute Trail. He had come deliberately hunting death and he'd found it.

Things don't always work out exactly right.

Ruff would have given a nickel to know if that man had a body that was covered with tattoos.

5

The valley was quite beautiful, crowded with tall spruce and pockets of quaking aspen just starting to go golden and red. The high peak was like a purple wall just across the valley, so high and sheer and barren was it. Below and to either shoulder, smaller peaks spread out, like rows of dragon teeth. Down in the heart of the valley was the dirty little collection of buildings they called Hardship.

Ruff pulled up his collar and started on down. Beside the trail a freshet hissed and gurgled its way downstream, running over rocks and twisted roots, foaming and misting. There was snow here and there in patches under the trees. The road Ruff was following now was little used, yet it was the main road into Hardship. There had to be some reason for the town's existence, but Ruff hadn't a clue as to what it was.

"Roland, you did choose a spot," he said musingly. No doubt it was beautiful, with eighty- to a hundred-foot trees stabbing at the sky and the ring of surrounding mountains, but there were other places nearer some sort of civilization just as beautiful.

Why, Justice wondered, had his brother settled here? The answer seemed to be very simple: he wanted to be as far away from people as possible.

"Hiding?" Ruff asked himself, and damn him if that wasn't exactly what it seemed.

He came around a bend in the trail, and there was the collection of used lumber they called Hardship, Colorado. Ruff rode right up to the store, Stokes' store, where a single mule stood hipshot at the bowed hitch rail. He swung down, looped the gray's reins over the rail, ducked under, and went on in. The big dog was content to stay outside on the boardwalk.

"Holy shit!" The man nearest the door almost fell down trying to get up from his barrel chair. He knocked the rickety table in front of him over, spilling a deck of greasy playing cards and a bottle of whiskey.

Ruff watched the man darkly, thinking at first that he was going for a gun. Then, puzzled, he simply stood frowning as the man cowered on the floor. Another man was coming across the store, this one wearing a big buffalo coat, although it wasn't very cold inside.

"Damn you, oh," the man on the floor moaned. "Don't do this to me. I didn't do anything to you."

"Get up, Andy," the man in the buffalo coat said sharply. "Damn you, get up and lay off that whiskey."

He yanked the man to his feet, but he stood there shuddering, gawking at Ruff Justice.

"What's the trouble?" Ruff asked.

"You—I helped bury you," Andy Buehler said, a pointing finger trembling.

"Mister," Ned Stokes said, "I apologize to you, but, you see, last year a man staggered through that door and he died here. Damn me if you're not a ringer for him. You've got to be Roland Justice's brother."

"That's right, I am. And you're Ned Stokes?"

"That's me, such as I am. Come on over to the bar and I'll pour you a whiskey. I could use one myself."

"You have one. I don't drink."

"No? Andy pull yourself together. For God's sake, this isn't the same man! There's a good recommendation for not drinking, I'll tell you," Stokes said. "Funny thing, I recollect your brother saying he didn't drink either. That was when the pain got real bad and I wanted to give him something to take the edge off of it."

"No, Roland didn't drink."

"What is it, some religion?"

"A promise," Ruff Justice told him. "Back a long ways."

"Well, that's something. A man that keeps his word is rare. You don't mind?" Ruff said he didn't and Stokes poured himself a huge glass of whiskey. He was a big-shouldered, ratty man in a ratty buffalo-hide coat, his fingernails black, his face unshaven, eyes red and bleary. He was, he told Ruff, the reason Hardship was there.

"I got tired of moving, so I stopped. I had in mind to start a store in California. Well, dammit, I refused to budge, and they couldn't make me—the other folks in the wagon train. I planted myself here and started my store. I guess I'm going slowly broke, but you don't get out of this life rich anyway, do you?"

"No, I don't suppose so."

"No. Dammit, Andy, what's wrong now?" Stokes shouted at Buehler. He was peering out the smoky window almost in terror, his small body quivering.

"Wolf," he hissed, "there's a wolf out on the stoop, Ned."

"Dammit, Andy!" Buehler was going to have to be limited on those drinks, Stokes thought as he poured himself another. "There ain't no wolf gonna walk down and sit on the damned stoop of my store."

"It's a dog," Ruff Justice said.

"Your dog?"

Ruff shrugged. "It's traveling around with me. It's anybody's dog, if I can find someone willing to feed it."

"There, you hear that, Andy? Just Mister Justice's dog."

That didn't settle Andy Buehler much. A dead man walking around with a wolf in tow was just a little much to be explained away easily. He picked up the spilled bottle, eyeing it to see what might be left, and sat down to the table, diligently going at it.

"You'll be wanting to know about your brother," Stokes said.

"Yes. That's right."

"Well." Stokes rubbed his jaw energetically. "What we know was mostly in that letter Handy Cross wrote. Some of us was sitting around here the day of our first blizzard last year, and in staggers this tall man with— Well, he was your brother. I tried to have María—she's the help—take a look at him, but it wasn't any use. It was a gunshot, close up and low down into the guts."

"Anybody save the bullet?"

"Huh? No, we didn't worry none about anything like that. It was a big slug, though, I'll tell you that." Stokes knocked back another drink of whiskey. Ruff was beginning to wonder how he stayed on his feet and how he could be cold enough to wear that buffalo coat.

"Did he say anything?" Ruff wanted to know.

"No. Not really. Like who shot him? No. He just told us it was a gunshot wound, which anyone could see, and then he sat down and died." Stokes nodded. "Right over there next to the stove."

"He had enemies around here?"

Stokes shook his head. "Not that I'd know about. We hardly ever seen the man. He was a loner. Had his place up over the hogback—I never even seen it. Someone said he had some horses, but I wouldn't even know about that myself."

"Who would?" Ruff asked.

"Huh? Well, I don't know. King Forrest has all that land up on the hogback, most of the deep valley across the ridge. He runs cattle. He was the nearest neighbor, I'd guess. Maybe Forrest might know. King Forrest get those horses, Andy?"

Andy didn't answer. He'd fallen asleep.

"Can you tell me how to find my brother's place?"

"I can tell you approximate, sure. Like I say, I never been there myself. Don't care for wandering around much." Stokes winked heavily. "I'll sketch you a little map. Won't be much to see, though."

"No, I guess not. Tell me, did you ever see a tattooed man around these mountains."

"See him? Yes, I reckon I did. Cold-blooded bastard."

"Hard one, was he?"

"Yes, I'll say. Came in here one night all dressed in black like Satan himself. He walked right over here and pulled off his gloves—tattoos all over his hands. Come to think of it . . . why, he was asking where Roland Justice could be found."

There was a little more conversation, but Stokes was off in his own world, and although generally a storekeeper in a settlement like Hardship knows most of what's going on, Stokes was the exception. He had his half-dozen cronies and his whiskey, and the rest of the world could rot for all he cared.

Ruff went out into the cold clear light of day, and the dog got to its feet, tail thumping against the side of the building. Ruff scratched its head absently.

He didn't like this; he wasn't sure there was any way of finding out what had happened nearly a year ago. The tattooed man was taking on the dimensions of a myth. Likely he had been nothing more sinister than an old seafaring mate of Roland's.

"Let's ride," Ruff said to the dog, which seemed eager enough to be moving again. Its shoulder had healed remarkably well, considering the lack of rest the animal had had, and it was fattening up, its gray wolf coat growing sleek.

Ruff swung aboard his horse, looked to the mountains for his landmarks, and started out of town. He didn't make it.

The rifle bullet clipped saddle leather from beneath his hand. Ruff Justice flung himself to the ground as the horse reared in fright, tossing its head.

The rifle fired again as Ruff landed. He saw several things simultaneously. The glint of sunlight on a rifle barrel, curling smoke marking the marksman's position; the horse running away up the street; heads poking out of Stokes' store, then rapidly withdrawing.

The dog had taken off in a beeline toward the rifleman and a hurried shot spattered dirt up into the animal's face. It didn't slow the dog down one bit. It knew that the gun meant danger. It knew all about guns and bows and arrows and man-war. And it didn't have any fear left. After passing by death close enough that happens. It happens to a man who figures he is living on free time; it had apparently happened to the dog. The bullets didn't frighten it, nor did the bellow of the rifle.

The sniper fired again at the dog. He should have paid more attention to the man in buckskins, the man with the long hair and the big blue Colt. Ruff Justice lifted his pistol and double-handed it, his hair in his eyes, his guts hot with anger—he had never liked people trying to put him under the ground where the sun didn't shine on you in the mornings. He wasn't a quick-draw specialist, but he had put more than a round or two through that long-barreled Colt.

He put one more through now. The Colt bucked in his hands, kicking his arms up. Smoke wreathed Ruff Justice. The gunman in the alleyway went back and down, sprawling against the alley before the dog had reached him.

Ruff started that way, holding his hat in one hand, his Colt in the other. The dog stood snuffling around the body. Ned Stokes and Buehler were coming at an ungainly run, several other townspeople behind them.

The dog looked up at Ruff, its yellow eyes glazed with ferocity, but Ruff settled it with a hand on the head.

"No. Good boy. Sit down there now." The dog surprised him by sitting. Someone had done a good job of training it. Ruff supposed that when you had a dog that big, you had better train it well.

"What happened?" It was a man Ruff had never seen, a wheezing, balding man in shirt sleeves.

"Man mistook me for an Indian."

"Who is it?" This was Ned Stokes, crowding forward into the dark, muddy alley.

"You'll have to tell me," Ruff said.

"Never saw him before. You, Al?"

"Never," the bald man said.

Ruff hunkered down and started going through the dead man's pockets, finding nothing. The sniper wore gloves. Ruff peeled one off, but there were no tattoos underneath.

"We can't have this," someone was chirping. "There'll have to be a trial. We just can't have people shooting each other in the middle of the street."

"Why don't you go ahead and do that?" Ruff said, standing to tower over the speaker. "Have your trial and let me know how it turns out." To Stokes he said, "Can you get someone to bury him for me?" He handed the man two silver dollars.

Then he walked to the waiting gray, which was skittish just now, climbed aboard, and rode slowly out of Hardship, the wolf dog at his horse's heels.

Ruff was bothered now. That man hadn't trailed him from the other side of the mountains. He had been there in Hardship, waiting. And when he saw Ruff, he had opened up.

The explanations were few. Perhaps he had been mistaken for Roland—although everyone in Hardship seemed to know he was dead; or, and this seemed more likely, everyone knew that Roland had had a brother and that Handy Cross had written him a letter.

Why? Why did they want to kill Ruff? Why kill Roland? What had he had? The ranch—a small one, by all accounts. The horse herd with his blooded Morgan stallion? Valuable enough in its own right. Or was it a grudge of long standing?

"The nearer I get the less I know," Ruff muttered. There was too much going on he didn't understand. He knew only one thing for certain: they wanted him dead. Whoever they were, whatever else they wanted, they wanted Ruff Justice dead.

Maybe King Forrest could tell him why.

He meant to see the man as soon as possible. He was riding now over land that had belonged to Roland. And on it were cattle wearing a brand that was a sort of crown with an "F" superimposed. Did that mean Forrest had this land legally now? What else was going on in these mountains? Ruff had heard of a good-sized gold strike up here, one no one was talking about. The gold, nearly jewelers' grade, just came down and was sold. The site of the mine was a secret; although a few men had tried to follow the couriers back, no one had succeeded.

A gold claim? Reason enough to kill, but no one seemed to be working a claim around here, not one of any size at least—there were none of the distinctive sounds, metal against stone, the sounds of digging. But then maybe the men who had killed Roland were patient enough to wait until all possible opposition was out of the way—like a brother who might have legal rights to the claim.

The cabin sat on the hillside in the shadows of the great pines. Ruff sat the ridge and looked down at it, across the snow-patched meadow. It was a pretty and private place, peaceful and protected from the harshest winds.

"You chose well, brother," Ruff said. He started

the gray down the slope toward the cabin, feeling for the first time a real pang of loss.

There was a grave there, near the house, although Roland had been buried down below in Hardship. There was a grave, and someone beside it.

6

Ruff Justice swung down and led his horse forward across the long grass meadow toward the house where Roland had lived. The grave was beneath a lone aspen, and around it were freshly planted flowers.

The dark-haired woman was standing there, her head bowed. At Ruff's approach she turned her head, and he had a glimpse of a pretty face, dark-eyed with long eyelashes, a small, narrow nose with slightly flaring nostrils, and full lips.

She stood staring at Ruff for a moment. Then her mouth opened and she said a single word.

"You . . ." Then she fainted dead away, falling across the grave before Ruff could catch her.

He dropped the reins to the gray, scooped her up, and walked toward the cabin. She was very light, very well put together, he noticed. Her breasts were nicely molded, hardly concealed by the dark dress she wore. Her face was pale now, childlike, but even more attractive close up.

Ruff kicked open the door to the cabin and went in. There was a bed in the corner. Dusty, the mattress rolled back, the frame was made of rough timbers and leather strapping. He put the girl there, letting her head rest on the mattress, which was very thin, stuffed with straw.

Ruff crossed the room then and opened the window, which had real glass in it. Eight little panes. Or seven—one of them had been broken out.

"Go on out," he told the dog, which had followed them in. It cocked its head curiously and then turned and padded toward the door.

Ruff walked back to where the girl lay. He patted her hand a little, but that didn't do any good. He frowned and went outside himself, looking for a well but finding none. Roland hadn't been that worried about the conveniences, apparently. He was carrying his water from somewhere and Ruff couldn't guess where.

He walked back toward the house, pausing to look down across the meadow toward the clouds that had settled in the valleys below him, toward the distant hazy plains. From here a man could see anyone coming for miles—a good reason to build here if you were expecting company you didn't want.

Ruff saw the bullet scar in the cross timber above the door. A .44 or larger had tunneled into the header, digging out scores of jagged splinters. If the line of sight was followed, it went back to the broken windowpane.

"It happened here," Ruff said. "Right here."

He went inside and sat beside the bed, waiting for the woman to come around.

Five minutes later, her eyelids fluttered open and she lay staring at the ceiling, dazed and lost. "What is this?" she asked. "I was . . ."

Then she sat up suddenly, her eyes turning to meet the gaze of Ruff Justice. Her mouth fell open, her fingertips went to her breast.

"You!" she said in a half-whisper.

"Please." Ruff smiled gently. "My name is Ruffin Justice. My brother lived here . . . and died here."

"God," she breathed. "I thought . . . Well, what else would a person think? Here, thinking of him . . . I'm sorry, I'll be all right in a minute."

"Just take it easy," Ruff said. "I didn't mean to startle you out there."

"I was thinking ... he was so near to me in thoughts, and then to have you pop up, you can't imagine what it was like." She smiled, but weakly.

"Sorry," Ruff repeated. "What is that grave doing out there anyway? They told me he was buried down in town."

"Yes. In back of the store. That's not where he would have wanted to lie."

"No."

"He would have wanted to be here. In the mountains. It's so lovely here. Especially in the spring, when the flowers dot the meadows ..." She blushed.

"You liked him a lot."

"We were ... close. I loved him."

"I don't think I got your name," Ruff Justice said. The girl had turned her eyes away. Now she looked back, touching her hair nervously with her pale fingers.

"Natalie Forrest."

"King Forrest's daughter?"

"His niece. But how did you know ... ?"

"It's a small area. People mention names. I saw your uncle's stock grazing down below and ..."

"Yes?" she asked brightly, her head tilted.

"Nothing."

"That was a question, or becoming one. Oh, I see—no! How could you think such a thing?"

"What sort of thing?" Ruff asked innocently.

"That my uncle could have murdered Roland."

"I didn't say that."

"You wondered. And what for?"

"For the graze? The land? I don't know."

"No, you don't know. Grass is cheap around here, mister. There's not much stock around."

"No. Not here," Ruff said. "I don't see any Morgan horses, for one thing."

"Is that it?" She laughed harshly. "You want the stallion. That's why you've come up here."

"Where is it now?" Ruff asked. The girl wasn't hysterical by any means, but she was pretty well worked up. He couldn't blame her much, the way he had just appeared out of nowhere, and it hadn't exactly been tactful to mention her uncle's name in connection with the incident. But then he didn't think being tactful was going to solve this thing for him.

"The stallion," Natalie Forrest sniffed, "is on the Forrest ranch, where it belongs. Roland wanted me to have it, if anything happened to him, and so I have it. And I must say that he was much more the gentleman than you appear to be, Mister Ruffin Justice!"

"Likely. Did he talk much about that?"

"Pardon me?"

"You said he wanted you to have the stallion, if anything happened to him. Did he talk much about that possibility? About the chance that something might happen?"

"You know." Natalie looked thoughtful. She sat with her hands clasped in her lap, facing Ruff, her large dark eyes on his. "He did, actually. Not to the point of being morbid or anything, but he spoke of death quite a bit."

"As if he expected to die."

"Yes." She nodded. "Exactly. I hadn't really thought of it like that. But it was almost as if he expected . . . this."

Tears had collected in her eyes and Ruff waited until she had gotten ahold of herself, dabbing the tears away with a knuckle. Then he asked, "What about the tattooed man?"

"What?" She looked blank. "I don't know what you mean. Did you say tattooed man?"

"Yes. Didn't Roland say anything about a tattooed man?"

"No, nothing to me. Why? What does that have to do with it?"

"I don't know," Justice said. "I really don't."

"It's getting on," she said suddenly. "I suppose I ought to be riding home. They'll wonder where I've gotten off to."

"Mind if I ride along?"

"Whatever for?"

"I'd just like to see where your uncle's ranch is. Besides, there may be Utes out prowling."

"They never come up this far."

"They never did before. They never went down as far as Bent Creek until last month either. They've got a new war leader who wants to spread out a little."

"I don't scare easily, Mister Justice."

"No?"

Her dark eyes glistened and she met his gaze with an expression he couldn't quite fathom. She was a deep one, Ruff would have bet. All the same, it was easy to see why Roland had fallen for her—if he had. She had said that she loved him. Was that the same as saying Roland loved her, or not? They went outside and stood looking at the grave while the drifting clouds shadowed the long valley below.

"Is that your dog?" Natalie asked, nearly shuddering at the sight of it.

"Do you need one? I've been trying to get rid of him since we met."

"Get rid of him?" Natalie turned those large liquid eyes on Ruff. "Why, you just can't turn a dog away after it's offered you friendship."

Ruff started to smile, but the woman was dead serious. He shrugged and started walking with her toward her horse, which had been left up in the cool pines.

"What's his name?" Natalie asked.

"Who?"

"The dog, of course."

"No name."

"That's a crime, Ruff Justice. You have to let it have a name, an identity."

"I'll think on it."

He helped her aboard her sorrel pony, then swung up on his little gray. They hadn't discussed it anymore, but when she started out homeward, Ruff just rode along. The dog trailed after, as always.

Ruff looked over the land of tall, pine-clad peaks interrupted by grassy high valleys. Here and there cattle grazed, and there were horses in a small tight bunch. None of them looked to have Morgan blood. Just what, Justice wondered, was that stallion worth? He had heard of one going for a hundred thousand dollars in a North Carolina sale. Was Roland's worth anything like that?

"You can see the house now. Over there, through the valley."

Ruff squinted that way, making out little more than a whitish blur. It was a lovely long valley, however, and the man that owned that was fortunate indeed. As they drew nearer, he could see white fences, horses grazing placidly, a grove of huge old spruce trees clustered around the white house protectively. A narrow silver creek ran across the long valley and a bridge had been built across it where the path met it.

"Very fancy."

"Uncle needed the bridge for his buggy. He doesn't ride anymore. His legs are not much good."

"Did Roland get over this way much?"

She looked at him quickly. "Not much."

"Why not?"

"I don't know."

"Didn't he get along with King Forrest?"

"I suppose not. Uncle wanted the little parcel of land Roland had. But . . ." Her eyes widened with awareness. "There was nothing like that between them. Really."

"Really?" Ruff smiled thinly. Now King Forrest had the Morgan horse; soon he would have the land. Ruff wasn't ready to judge the man guilty on that alone, but it did give him cause to wonder.

They were into the shadow of the big white house now. A Chinese in apron and cap stood on the porch watching their approach, then he went rather excitedly inside. Off to the right Ruff saw a row of new white paddocks. There the Morgan would be kept, he supposed. Beyond that was a bunkhouse, low, of unpeeled log construction, built, at a guess, for a dozen men. Beyond that the forest closed out the view, but from somewhere higher up the slope smoke rose. Maybe a blacksmith's shop, Ruff was thinking.

The door to the house burst open and a big man with a gun strapped around his ample waist stepped out. He was thick-shouldered, the color of raw beef. He had on twill pants stuffed into high boots and a blue cotton shirt with the sleeves turned back over enormous forearms.

Even from that distance Ruff heard the man breathe a curse, saw his hand rest on the butt of his holstered pistol.

"Who's that?"

"Dirk. John Dirk. He's the foreman."

"He seems glad to see me."

"Ruff—you just don't realize how much you look like your brother. If it weren't for that mustache, you'd be a dead ringer. It's startling, believe me."

"All right," Ruff said, "it's not me Dirk doesn't like. It's Roland."

The lady didn't offer any argument.

"Thank you for escorting me," she said.

"Turning me away?"

"I thought you just wanted to see me home."

"I did. Mind if I swing down for a while, though? I'm getting a little saddle-sore."

"It's not a good idea. I'd invite you in to dinner, but . . . It's just not a very good idea, Ruff."

"All right. Mind if I see the Morgan, then?"

They had halted their horses thirty feet from the porch. John Dirk stood there staring at them, trying to overhear their conversation.

It took Natalie some time to answer. "Why? Why do you want to see the horse?"

"What's wrong with that?" Ruff asked. "It seems natural enough to me."

"Well, I'm sure you could look at it."

"Besides," he added, "I'll probably want to take it with me."

"You can't!"

"Sure I can."

"But he's Unc—mine. Roland wanted me to have him."

"I know you said that, Natalie, but I think maybe we ought to keep it in the family. Does it mean that much to you?"

"Yes, of course . . ." Her head hung. Her sentence trailed off feebly.

"What did Roland tell you about the Morgan stallion?"

"Nothing. He didn't give it to me. Uncle told me to say that to people."

"If you want—"

"I'm not going to beg you for the horse!" she spat. "I don't really care. All I cared about was Roland— and about keeping other people from getting hurt."

"Like me?"

"Like you. What would have happened if you rode in here with the idea that Uncle King had stolen the Morgan."

"The same thing that's going to happen now, I suppose," Ruff Justice said. He nodded toward the porch. A grizzled man leaning on one crutch, supported on the other side by a kid of eighteen or twenty stood there. A mat of white hair showed in the V of his white shirt. He was rugged, square-cut, his jowels just beginning to sag. Oh, he had been a man in his prime, had King Forrest. You only had to look at him to see that was so. Big, broad, taking what he wanted from life.

He had taken one item too many. And if he had taken Roland Justice's life, he would be taking nothing more at all.

Natalie swung down and walked her horse toward the porch. Ruff followed suit, his eyes on the old man, on John Dirk, who looked ready to go to knuckles or knives or six-guns as Ruff preferred.

"Uncle King. This is Roland's brother, Ruffin Justice. He's ridden all the way from Dakota Territory."

"He can ride right back, as far as I'm concerned," King Forrest said inhospitably. It didn't look to Ruff as if they were destined to become fast friends. "What are you doing with my niece and what are you doing on my property?" he demanded.

"Brought the girl home. Want my brother's horse," Ruff answered directly.

"You what?" King Forrest started stuttering, trying to move forward toward Justice, though the kid beside him was sorely pressed to support him. "What the hell horse do you mean? Natalie, get in the house. Now."

"The Morgan," Ruff said, watching Natalie hoist her skirts and dutifully head for the door of the big white house. "I have heard there's more than one horse, though, thirty or forty of them maybe missing. So I guess I'll just take them all along, but mainly it's the Morgan I wanted."

"Well, he's gone. He was stolen," King Forrest snapped. "As for the rest of the horses, I never saw them."

"Maybe I could look around."

"I'll settle him, boss," John Dirk said in a low, barely human voice. He started forward, but King Forrest halted him with a single word.

"No. Anyway," he said to Justice, "that Morgan

horse was given to my niece. She ought to have told you that."

"Oh, she told me that, all right," Ruff answered.

"And what? You calling her a liar?"

"I wouldn't mind seeing it written down some-where," Ruff answered.

"Greedy, is that it? You want those horses bad, don't you?"

"If they're gone, I don't see what you care. I don't see what it matters if I take a look around either."

"What it matters!" King Forrest exploded. "Why, it amounts to calling me a liar and a thief, don't it?"

"Dad . . ." The kid beside Forrest began, but King Forrest back-handed the kid viciously across the mouth and he staggered backward, nearly falling.

From around the corner of the house two more men came. Both were lean and mustached—there the resemblance ended. One was hook-nosed, red-headed, dressed in flannels and twills. The other was dark, sporting a narrow mustache. He was in black jeans and a black silk shirt. One sleeve had a silver garter on it. He was wearing twin Colts. The man obviously fancied himself. He tried lounging casually against the porch upright.

"I think you ought to get off my property right now," King Forrest said, and Ruff, looking over the five men he faced, was inclined to agree.

"Does that mean there's no supper invite?" Justice asked dryly. The redhead laughed and Forrest shot him a hard glance. The kid who was holding him up, Forrest's son, had blood trickling from his nose. The would-be gunman still lounged, his thumbs hooked in his gunbelt.

"Get off my place," King Forrest repeated. "And stay off the RJ too—that's mine now."

"The RJ—that's my brother's brand, is it?"

"It was."

"Good. I'll be able to identify any stock that's missing that way." He swung up onto the gray, which sidestepped a little. "But as far as getting off Roland's place goes, forget it. If you've got a good deed, let's see it now and I might consider it. If you don't, it seems pretty clear that I've got a better claim than you'll ever have. To that land—and to the Morgan stallion."

"Damn you . . ." King started sputtering again, but Ruff just turned the gray and went loping off, the dog following him. After his horse had clattered across the little bridge fording the creek, Ruff let out his breath. He should quit playing these games—sooner or later someone was going to call his bluff.

He rode slowly homeward, watching sunset color the sky with crimson battle flags. The pines drew together and huddled darkly along the mountain slopes.

Ruff Justice was riding home now—home to the cabin, that is, to Roland's home. The place must have meant a lot to him. He had chosen his spot and built well. But then they had come and cut him down. For that they would pay, and it didn't matter who it was that had done it.

The whole thing puzzled Ruff and just now he didn't have a handle on it. No less puzzling was the fact that there was smoke rising from the chimney of Roland's cabin.

7

It didn't belong, but there it was—smoke curling up against the sundown sky from Roland Justice's stone chimney. Ruff held up the gray and sat scowling for a moment, wondering. He couldn't see any horse, but one could easily have been concealed in the pines.

"Well, if they're trying to hide, they're doing a damn poor job of it," he said to the dog. "Let's go on down and see what we've got."

Darkness was falling fast, and as Ruff emerged from the pines again minutes later, there was only a pale pinkish pennant in a dark sky to mark the passing of the sun. The cabin was fire-lit. Reddish yellow at the windows, sparks sputtering from the chimney, gold and red against the night. Ruff still saw nothing.

To the north those big-footed, creeping thunderheads rumbled and grumbled a little, but that was the only sound across the dark and empty mountain.

Ruff swung down, palming his Colt. Leaving the gray where it stood, he walked toward the cabin, coming up on the side away from the door. The dog came along, going to its belly, taking it all for a hunting game perhaps.

But Ruff wasn't taking it for a game. People had

been killed in these mountains, and they had tried to put him in that category this afternoon.

Reaching the cabin, he lifted up and peered sideways into the window. There was nothing to see. Shifting a little to the other side, he could see that the bed had been made up. There was a picnic basket on the table, a cloth spread over it.

"They bring gifts," Ruff muttered.

He walked to the front door and entered. The blonde sat near the fire in the rocking chair, her booted ankles crossed, a green shawl over her shoulders.

"Well, damn near time," she drawled.

"Sorry." Ruff holstered his Colt and took off his hat. The girl kept right on rocking. She had merry blue eyes, and her hair, which reached to her waist, was done up in one long braid. She wore men's pants and a cotton shirt, blue-checked. Her breasts filled it out nicely and she caught Ruff's eyes on her and gave a disparaging laugh.

"Just a man, is that it?"

"That's it."

"Like 'em?" she asked.

"Yes, as a matter of fact."

"I'll show 'em to you sometime." She got up from the chair, walked to Ruff, and looked him up and down with frank appraisal. Then she stuck out her hand and said, "Sue Blackcastle."

"Ruffin T. Justice."

"What's the T for?"

"Trouble, they say." Her hand was as callused as a man's. She had a grip on her, too.

"I'll bet they do. Just like your brother, is that it?"

"I don't know. I haven't seen him much."

"Well, you won't see him again."

"No."

Her hand fell away and she turned back toward the fire—but not before Justice saw the mist begin to gather in those bright-blue eyes. She wasn't all that tough.

"Mind if I ask what you're doing here?" Ruff asked.

"Just cozying up for you. Thought I'd set a spell and wait. I wanted to take the basket back if you showed up to eat. Ned Stokes sent me up. Said you wouldn't be feeding yourself. Christ, what's that?"

Ruff knew without looking behind him. "Just a dog."

"I got a grizzly hide at home smaller than that. And believe me, it wasn't no cub."

"You work for Stokes, do you?"

"Yeah." She turned and crouched down, tossing her shawl onto the rocker. "Sort of."

"But you knew Roland."

"I didn't say that. No, I didn't know him."

Ruff looked into her eyes, not quite believing something about this one. "What's in the basket?"

"Aw, just some chicken and biscuits. You know."

"Will you join me?"

"Huh? No. I don't eat my own cooking."

"Whose, then?"

"That was just a joke, you know." Sue swung around, stuck her legs out flat on the floor, and leaned back on her hands. The firelight painted subtle highlights in her blond hair. "Don't you know a joke when you hear one?"

"Sure. I just haven't been laughing much lately." Ruff sat down at the table facing the girl. "If you don't mind," he said, and helped himself to a chicken leg. His hat was on the table and his other hand was near his gun. Not that anything seemed wrong, but you never knew. After all, another man had been killed in this cabin, and a woman could have done the job.

"Any good?" she asked.

"Not bad at all," Ruff answered. His mind was on something else. Sue might have come up here to clean up and offer a little mountain hospitality, but she had also taken the time to search the cabin. At least Ruff thought so. The picture on the wall had been crooked earlier when Natalie Forrest was there. The bed had been moved as well. Ruff could see the marks where the legs had been. Interesting.

"Talkative, ain't you?" Sue said.

"Sometimes," Justice said.

"Well, I guess it's no fun for you right now."

"Very little." He continued to chew thoughtfully, to watch. He asked, "How long did you know Roland?"

"Say, didn't I say I never knew the man? What is this, some game or something?"

"Absentmindedness."

"Sure." She was quite a moment before she asked, "Just about ready to head back for the flatlands, are you?"

"Not quite, no."

"I mean, I figured maybe you had your business just about taken care of."

"No," Ruff said. "I don't."

Sue made a small noise, like a disgusted clearing of the throat, but Ruff wasn't sure what it meant. She got suddenly to her feet, snatched up her shawl as if he'd insulted her deeply, and started toward the door. "I got to go now."

"Wait awhile and take your basket."

"You keep the goddamned thing," Sue Blackcastle said, and then she was gone, slamming the door shut.

Ruff got to his feet and strolled to the door. By the time he had stepped outside, she was gone, riding up through the pines on a horse he couldn't make out well enough to identify.

He grinned. "Mountain cat, are you?" He shook his head and started back toward the house. It was then that he noticed the grave. Someone had taken the flowers Natalie had put there and ripped them up, crushing them to barren stalks and torn petals.

Ruff looked again to the pines and then walked to

the grave, crouching down to look it over. Someone with a savage hatred had done this. He picked up a crushed flower and shook his head again.

"Who is it she hates, Roland? You or the other woman?"

He went back inside the cabin, sat down, and finished the chicken and biscuits, thinking that whoever had made it was a pretty good cook—or at least seemed so after a week of antelope.

After eating, Ruff poked around a little himself, trying to imagine what Sue Blackcastle could have been looking for. His guesses ranged from incriminating letters or pieces of ladies' clothing to maps to secret mines, deeds, a will . . . He let his imagination run rampant, since he had no real idea at all. All he did know was that it was small enough to be hidden in the cabin.

Which left out what Ruff was after. He was going on a treasure hunt himself a little later, and he meant to come back with a Morgan stallion with "RJ" stamped on its butt.

He let the fire burn low as he shifted the bed, tested the fireplace for loose stones, tapped at the floor, chinned himself to look up in the loft above the ceiling, turned the picture on the wall once more, and shrugging, gave it up.

Maybe she got it already, he thought. It—whatever the hell it is, or was, or might be.

She might have gotten it, but Ruff thought not. One thing he was fairly sure of: Sue Blackcastle had come up to the house for just that purpose. She had brought along a picnic basket full of chicken as camouflage in case she met Justice. She had had her look-see, and then, hearing or suspecting Ruff was coming, she had boldly plopped down in the rocker and come out with her story.

"Which doesn't tell me what she wanted." Ruff sat down on the bed and put his boots up. "Dog, I don't like this business. I'm no good at mysteries. I like something I can grab hold of with both hands, test my strength against, win or lose with. This flitting around after ghosts I do not like at all. Just what in the hell is it they all want?"

The dog hadn't the faintest idea. While the fire burned low, Ruff lay back, closing his eyes to catch a few hours' sleep. The gray was outside, the dog near the threshold. No one would be sneaking up on him.

He fell asleep and dreamed of a tribe of Indians with tattooed bodies all riding big black Morgan horses. It wasn't all that restful.

When he awoke, the cabin was still and cool. There were just a few golden embers still alive in the hearth. He took a moment to look around, to come alert. Everything was all right. The dog was still there on watch. No one was around.

He stepped to the door and glanced at the Big Dipper. It was nearly three in the morning by the stars. Just right for what he had planned.

He went back in, slapping his arms. It was cold out there. The storm clouds had receded again, but they were lurking in the skies like great cat's paws toying with the mountain dwellers. It would snow.

"You are going to have to stay here, dog. Do you know what that means? Stay."

The dog had lifted its great head in anticipation, but now it slumped back and Ruff patted it.

"Yes, you know. All right." He picked up his hat and went out, leaving his buffalo coat, although it was bitter cold. He wanted the freedom of movement. For the same reason he had left his sheathed Spencer rifle in the house. He didn't worry about anyone taking it. They'd have to tangle with that dog in there to do it.

The gray looked at Justice as if he were crazy, but he stood for the saddle. He fought the bit a little and Ruff didn't blame him.

Ten minutes later he was riding through the pines in the cold dark night, the wind chanting in the

trees, the horse' hooves whispering over the pine
needles underfoot.

When he reached the Forrest ranch, it was dark.
There wasn't a lamp to be seen, not in the big house,
nor in the bunkhouse or any of the outbuildings. He
was up too early for even the Chinese cook to be
stirring. That didn't mean there wasn't a guard or
two posted.

"Wasn't too smart to make a brag like that, Ruffin
T.," he told himself. If the man wanted that horse as
bad as Forrest seemed to, he would have it protected.

Justice circled wide to the south and came back
along a little ridge he had spotted that afternoon.
From there he could see the back of the house. Still
dark, nothing stirring. Maybe.

He rode down to within a quarter of a mile, where
he dismounted. In that stillness, down the canyon
the sound of a horse walking, however lightly, would
carry.

Justice tied the reins to a small twig and started off
through the trees, his feet and hands cold, his nose
frozen, his mustache frosted. "Damn fool," he muttered to himself once. He got no argument.

He could see the white paddocks now. He heard a
horse blow and shift its feet. There was no other
sound. Ruff glanced at the skies. Still dark, the fickle
clouds moving in again. He stayed where he was,
crouched behind a screen of live oak for a long ten
minutes while his muscles stiffened and his blood
seemed to stop flowing in his veins.

Still it was a good thing he had waited.

He spotted the guard on the roof of the paddock,
and by looking carefully he picked up the other one
near the bunkhouse. They were signaling to each
other—that was what had caught Justice's eye in the
first place. They didn't seem to be trying to commu-
nicate anything important. Kid stuff, mostly.

"Clowns," Ruff muttered. MacEnroe would chew

them up in no time. But then these weren't soldiers; they were just cowhands trying to earn a buck.

He gave it a few more minutes to try to spot anyone else who might be around, but that was it. Just the two of them. Ruff moved in.

The man at the corner of the bunkhouse was first. He had to be; he was easy. Ruff's only concern was waking up the men sleeping inside the bunkhouse. A little noise and Ruff would be dead. There wasn't any noise.

The man was crouched down, making silly hand-talk to the guard on the roof. Ruff was standing behind him, his pistol raised. When the man on the roof of the stable took a half-turn away, Ruff Justice brought the barrel of his pistol down behind the cowboy's ear. He sighed and fell over. Ruff drew him back into the shadows, stripped off his coat and hat, and slipped into them.

Picking up the guard's rifle, he walked straight across the starlit yard to the paddock.

"What are you doing, Ed?" the man on the roof hissed. "We're not supposed to leave our posts."

Ruff made silly hand signs at the man and proceeded. He started at one end of the stable and walked slowly through it, seeing nothing but Crown-F brands.

The side door to the stable opened, creaking loudly. The man from the roof came up excitedly. "What in the hell are you doing here . . . Oh, shit!"

Ruff had a rifle leveled. The guard dropped his own weapon and his hands went up as if they had been burned.

"Where's the Morgan?"

"Not here."

"Don't lie to me, cowboy."

"I'm not lying," he replied, stuttering a little. Winchesters have been known to cause those slight speech impediments. "They took it out 'cause they thought you'd be coming in."

"Where'd they take it?"

"The high valleys. I don't know where exactly. Dirk took him up. Dirk and Sandy Forrest."

"The kid?"

"That's right."

"You wouldn't lie to me, would you, cowboy?" Ruff asked, and his voice must have sounded plain evil. Even by the feeble starlight bleeding through the stable windows Ruff could see that the man was pale and that he trembled.

"I'm not lying. I swear to God!"

"All right. Turn around and grip that post.'

"What're you going to do?"

"Turn around," Ruff repeated. He quickly tied the man, using the cowboy's own scarf and belt. He stuffed a balled handkerchief in his mouth and placed him in a stall. His friends were going to be kidding him for a long time, but it beat a bullet in the brain.

Ruff finished looking over the horses. There was nothing wearing an "RJ" brand there at all. A wasted night, and in the morning he would be lucky if they didn't come to pay him a return visit.

He started toward the door to find Natalie there, her hair down around her shoulders. She was staring, just staring as if she were asleep, her eyes open. She didn't seem to really see him, but her lips moved.

"Roland!"

"Wake up, Natalie. It's me. Ruff Justice."

"Roland," she said again, and then she was in his arms, holding him tightly, her hands running down his buttocks, up his thighs. Her head was thrown back, and the starlight showed the tears in her eyes.

"Listen, Natalie. Stop it now." Ruff took her hands away and stood staring down at her. "Wake up, girl! You remember me. Ruff Justice."

Then the knife flashed and Ruff had to leap back quickly. The silver blade cut past his belly and the girl threw back her head and let out a loud and eerie scream, a crazed shout.

"I've got him. I've got him!"

But she didn't. Ruff ducked under her arms and took off for his horse up the wooded slope. The bunkhouse doors had banged open as Natalie continued to shout and now a single shot was fired, high over Ruff's head, whining through the pines.

Ruff reached his gray and swung aboard. He rode a little higher up and looked back toward the Forrest Ranch. He could see a cluster of people there, but no one had a horse. The windows of the main house were lit up. Someone's bellowing voice carried indistinctly to Ruff's ears.

It was growing gray in the east. Dawn was breaking. It had been a bad night. Ruff Justice turned the gray toward home.

He was walking around in a nightmare. He couldn't figure out who was who. Who, if anyone, was on his side, on Roland's side?

He went back to the cabin, let the dog out, and boiled a pot of coffee while he listened for the sound of approaching horses. He had no idea what King Forrest was thinking, but it was very possible the man would be coming. With John Dirk. That one liked to hurt. There was Dirk and the gunman who liked to dress in black. They would be the ones to do the dirty work. But maybe they liked to have a mob at their heels to help out. Most men like that did.

Ruff had no sense of confidence in his own line of reasoning just now. He was a stranger, very visible, unsure of himself. The Morgan horse had been taken to a high valley—that meant nothing to Ruff. He figured he could spend the rest of his life looking around up there for a horse.

"Someone has got to come clean," he decided angrily. He threw the remainder of his coffee into the fire to hiss and steam. "Someone is going to tell me what the hell is going on around here."

He went out, closing the door, glancing at the trampled grave of Roland Justice. The grave in which he was not buried, but which Natalie kept as a monument. Natalie was another one—what the hell was she trying to do with that knife? Why? If she used a knife, could she use a gun on a man? And then mourn his death. Why not? A madwoman can do most anything.

Ruff gave up the wondering. He wanted someone to tell him flat out what was happening.

Dawn broke orange and crimson as Justice again rode out of the high valley. The gray was a little tired, the dog at his heels spry and energetic. Ruff tended to side with the horse. He was beginning to curse the day he had ridden into these tangled mountains.

Hardship slept in deep shadows as he rode toward the mountain town. He hoped Sue Blackcastle was an early riser. He hated to wake folks up.

8

When Ruff Justice swung down in front of Stokes' store, the owner himself was out front sweeping off the sagging porch with a raggedy broom. He wore his buffalo coat and a straw hat.

"Well, 'mornin', Mister Justice."

"Hello, Stokes."

"Got the beast with you, I see," he said, nodding at the dog. "What can I do for you? Need some supplies?"

"As a matter of fact, I do," Ruff answered. "But the main thing I need today is information."

"Come along inside and we'll see what we can do about both," Stokes answered. He yawned, turned, and went in, leaning his broom against the wall.

Andy Buehler was there already, and he was already drinking whiskey. And not just sipping it, but going at it thirstily, like he had just crawled in off the desert.

"What is it you wanted to know, Justice?"

"I need to talk to your girl."

"My girl?" Stokes took off his straw hat and scratched his head. "I got no girl, never did have."

"The one who works for you," Ruff said with less confidence.

"María?"

79

"No, the young one, Sue Blackcastle."

"I never even heard the name."

"Well, I didn't think she worked here, but she must live around here close. A blonde about so high, with a rugged way of talking, a little too much starch, wears a man's clothes."

"There's no one like that lives in these mountains, Mister Justice," Stokes told him. "No, sir, no one like that at all."

Justice bit at his lip in frustration. He had known something was wrong with the girl's story, but he figured she had to live in the area. She had apparently known Roland . . .

"I seen her."

It was Buehler who had spoken up, and Justice walked that way, looking down into the man's red eyes. "You saw the girl I described."

"Sure. Little feisty blonde. She was with the tattooed man."

"She was *what*? When was this?"

"Yesterday."

"You was in here all day yesterday, Andy," Ned Stokes said.

"No, I wasn't. Not when I went out back to see to my private business. I seen 'em then. Up the alley beside the livery. The girl, an old man, and the one with the tattoos. I knew him right off, Ned. Don't think I'd forget that black-eyed bastard, do you?"

"No, I guess not." Stokes said to Justice, "Well, there you are. If you can believe Andy—sometimes you can, sometimes you can't."

"How were they traveling?" Ruff asked.

"The old man and the girl in the wagon, a closed-in wagon, all of wood. The tattooed man, he was riding a big white horse. There was a pinto pony tied on back as well. I took that to be the girl's horse. Buy me a bottle, Mister Justice?"

"Sure. Did you talk to them?" Ruff gave Stokes a dollar for a bottle.

"Me? What for? Thank you, Mister Justice."

"Did they say anything, then? Warn you off?"

"Nope." Buehler cracked the new bottle. "But that tattooed man he don't have to say anything, Mister Justice. If you ever run into him, you'll see what I mean. He looks at you and those eyes say, Get. I got."

There wasn't any more to be learned from Buehler. Ruff bought a few supplies and went on out. He was more confused than when he rode into town. The livery barn was up two buildings and Justice went that way, leading the gray, the dog bouncing along happily. It was feeling frisky since the wound in its shoulder had almost healed. It also seemed to like this mountain air. Ruff himself hadn't gotten used to it. A change of altitude takes time.

"Yes? With you in a minute," the man in the livery barn called. He was working at his forge, hammering a horseshoe into shape.

"No hurry. Can we talk while you work?"

"Okay by me," the man answered. He was narrow, round-shouldered, nearly bald, with smudges of soot on his face. He banged the horseshoe with his hammer again. "What can I do you for?"

As Ruff came forward, the man's expression changed. "Oh, it's you. Didn't recognize you, Mister Justice. I got that spare branding iron for you if you want it."

"That was my brother," Ruff said.

"You know I thought . . . Yes, I heard about the other business. Sorry. My mind's wandering."

"I hope not too much. I wanted to ask you about something," Justice said, gesturing to the man to continue his work.

"Sure thing. Go ahead."

"I understand you had some customers yesterday from out of the area. A young woman, an older man . . ."

"And a man with tattoos. You're damned right. And what a wolf that one was!"

"What did they want?"

"They needed a tire for their wagon wheel, that's all. They threw it somewhere. But, God, you'd think they were in a race or something, the way they hurried me." He stopped and worked the bellows a few times, firing up the forge, which glowed cherry red, painting the smith's face crimson. He mopped it with his scarf.

"Did they mention their names?"

"Nope . . . Wait. The girl was called Sue, I believe. Not even sure of that, but I think so. None of the others mentioned a name."

"Did they say where they were going?"

"Nope, and I didn't care so long as they went. Odd bunch, they were."

"I'd say so." Ruff gave the man five dollars. "For that spare branding iron. I'd kind of like to have it. Can you bring it out for me?"

"Sure can. Say, I'm sorry about your brother." He wiped his hands on his leather apron and took the money. "I'll keep the iron here if you like. I'll get it. It's a good piece of work. I might not be too fast, but I'm generally credited with being neat."

"Sure," Ruff said with a slight smile.

The smith went to the corner of the shop and brought back the iron. It was beautifully made, the "RJ" twisting together in an intricate arrangment Roland must have designed. It made the letters resemble a knot—but then Roland had been a sailor, hadn't he?

"Nice. Very nice."

"Sure. Maybe you can use it one day."

"Maybe."

"Sure. Every man wants to have his own spread, his own horses. Well, I bet you've thought of settling down and owning your own ranch. Maybe you will."

"Maybe," Ruff said. He knew he didn't have that

sort of future, though. He had pushed cattle around before and didn't like it. The truth may have been that he didn't like working. He liked riding the long plains with the wind in his hair and a good horse beneath him; he liked the danger, the threat of the unknown, standing up to it and testing himself. When a man is made like that, he doesn't generally take too well to settling down. He doesn't generally live long enough to find out if he would have been any good at it.

He gave the iron back to the smith. He heard the door swing to behind him, and he was aware of the light of day being shut off, leaving the reddish glow of the forge. He turned toward the door to see John Dirk standing there, a shotgun in his hands.

" 'Morning, Justice," the big man said.

"Dirk."

"Heard you came to see us this mornin' but no one was up yet."

"No. It was another horse's ass I was looking for."

Dirk stiffened. That was all right. He wanted an excuse to do what he had come for, and Justice knew it. Why delay things? "I ought to kill you for that."

"Maybe. It wasn't real polite." Beside Dirk stood the kid, King Forrest's son, Sandy. He was not real confident. Behind Ruff Justice the smith was easing toward the side door.

"You know what this scattergun could do to you, Justice?"

"Yes," Ruff said calmly. "I've seen men with their hides full of buckshot. I've also seen plenty with a forty-four hole in their hearts. Some, I admit with a little shame, I've done it to myself."

And that was the situation exactly. Dirk could trigger off, but he was liable to take a bullet from that Colt in return.

"It's murder," Sandy Forrest said shakily. "Murder if you kill Ruff Justice."

"Why, he's a horse thief, Sandy," Dirk answered.

"No, he ain't. He never took no horse. Even Father couldn't protect you if you shot him down, Dirk."

"No? Maybe not. Maybe I don't need to shoot him down to teach him a lesson. What do you say, Justice? Shuck that Colt." Then Dirk tossed his shotgun to the kid, who caught it awkwardly. "Well?" Dirk was rolling up his sleeves, grinning crookedly. The man was enjoying himself. All that was missing was an audience—that was what John Dirk really wanted.

Ruff hated to disappoint the man. He unbuckled his Colt and hung his gunbelt over the stall nearby.

"I didn't think you had the guts, tall man," Dirk said. "I thought you were more like your brother—a coward."

The taunt didn't strike home. Ruff knew he was no coward, and he knew Roland Justice had not been one, either. The words meant nothing. Those big fists of John Dirk meant business, however.

"No more talking," Ruff said. "I don't much believe in that. You've got something to do, do it."

"Think you can do it," Dirk sneered. "Think you can, Mister Justice?"

"We'll know after a while. Come on—or are you all talk?"

That stung John Dirk. He really was thin-skinned for such a big, capable man. He charged across the livery barn, his fists windmilling, a roar emerging from his throat. He was determined to finish things quickly.

He didn't quite make it.

Ruff Justice stepped back and took a glancing blow from the big man's right hand on his shoulder, then uppercut with his own right. Dirk's head snapped back as knuckles met jawbone. Ruff had his back to the stable partition, and as Dirk continued in, cursing and swinging, Ruff lifted a leg and placed his foot in Dirk's belly, shoving hard.

The big man staggered back and Ruff Justice, his fists bunched, hair hanging in his eyes, waited.

"Dirk . . ." the kid said, but John Dirk ignored him and whatever he might have had to say. There was a thin trickle of blood leaking from Dirk's right nostril as he came in again, determined to tear Ruff's head off.

Justice was having none of it. He backed away, stabbing his left hand into Dirk's nose again and again as the big man pursued him, his eyes dark, his face sullen, glowering, just a little less than human.

"Kill you," Dirk muttered once, and there wasn't any doubt in Ruff's mind that he intended to do just that if he got the chance.

Dirk hooked with a left, missed with a right, and then connected with a left, a hard jolting blow that weakened Ruff's knees and drove him back.

Behind Ruff was an anvil mounted on a thick sawn log. Ruff came up against it sharply with the back of his legs, and before he could regain his balance, Dirk came in with a series of hard blows to the body, which Justice took. The third blow was the one that did it. A savage chop from Dirk's left dug into Justice's liver and filled his head with sparks of pain.

He folded up and heard Dirk roar with savage delight. The big man came in, hammering at his head with his meaty fists, but Ruff had enough presence of mind to roll away and get up on his toes, to jab constantly at Dirk's face as he drew away, circling.

The blows didn't do much damage. John Dirk swatted them away or ignored them completely as he plodded on in, his heavy arms hanging, his lip, puffed and purpled, curled back on one side.

"Come on, fancy man," Dirk growled. "Let's see what you're made of."

Justice laughed. Where the laugh came from he didn't know. But he threw his head back and let loose, although his insides hurt, a rib was possibly cracked, and his head rang with pain.

He laughed, and Dirk, enraged, came in again. But the big man's punches were losing their sting. He clubbed at Ruff's head and missed as Justice pulled back, tried to go to the wind, and had the blows blocked by Ruff's elbows.

Then he took Justice's stiff right and staggered back, his jaw gaping. Ruff didn't let him rest. He came in, stinging the big man with two rapid lefts then a right that crossed over and landed flush on Dirk's ear.

Blood leaked from the ear as Dirk twisted partly away, waving a feeble left hand at Justice, who was all over him now, mauling him like a big cat, the lefts going down to the ribs and then up to the head, the right working to the face and the heart when Dirk dropped his guard.

Dirk roared with pain and frustration. He threw himself at Justice, wrapping his bearlike arms around the scout, crushing him as he tried to knee Ruff's groin.

Justice dug his thumbs into the hollows beneath Dirk's ears and the big foreman fell back screaming with pain. He tried to claw at Ruff's face, to gouge his eyes as he stepped back, but Justice knocked the pawing hands away, kicking Dirk in the knee with the heel of his boot for good measure.

The foreman staggered away and then, yelling, hurled his body at Ruff's again. Ruff caught him coming in with a sharp right that landed on the neck just below the ear and Dirk went down. For perhaps the first time in his long career as a bully, John Dirk tasted dirt, tasted blood and felt the pain, the fear of defeat.

Defeat was unthinkable. His pride wouldn't allow it. Fear of defeat lifted him to his feet. Fear drove him into Ruff's darting, slashing fists.

Dirk might have been weary. There might have

been blood and sawdust, oil and dirt on his face, and he might have been wheezing like a steam boiler with a hole in it, but he wasn't going to quit, not just yet.

He got Ruff Justice once with a sledgehammer right that shook Ruff's teeth and sent him wobbling backward. Still he smiled, still he laughed, and Dirk, enraged by the mockery, came in incautiously.

For the last time.

Ruff fired off a left to the ribs, feinted with a right, and then lifted the left, hooking it into Dirk's face. It split the cheekbone wide open, spattering both men with blood. It landed flush, sending a message of surrender to the brain.

John Dirk's eyes rolled back and his head lolled on his neck for a moment. Then he simply nodded and went down. Ruff stepped aside to let him flop against the floor of the livery where he stayed, his damaged nose fluttering with his ragged breathing.

Justice turned back toward the partition and went for his Colt, but the kid spoke up just as he drew the gun from his holster.

"No," Sandy Forrest said. "I'm not in this, Mister Justice."

"Then toss that scattergun aside. That and your belt gun. I'd be obliged."

"Yes, sir." He did it with some alacrity. The guns clattered to the floor. The smith had emerged from some hidey-hole and now stood over the battered, bloody form of John Dirk.

"Damn me," he said, "I never thought I'd live to see this."

"It can happen to anybody, believe me," Ruff said. "Want to hand me that branding iron?"

"You're not going to . . ."

Ruff looked at the "RJ" iron, at the glowing forge, and then at the collapsed figure of John Dirk. The big man lay with his ample flank turned toward them.

"No." It was just too easy. "No, I just want the iron."

Ruff took it from the smith and went on out. He had swung aboard the gray before the kid caught up with him.

"Mind if I ride a ways with you?" Sandy asked. His eyes were childlike. There was still a bruise where his old man had backhanded him.

"What for?"

"We're headed the same way."

"Maybe."

"Look, Mister Justice, I'm not your enemy, and I wasn't Roland's. We were friends. I'd like to help you find who did it."

"That might strike awful close to home, kid."

"Yes," he said soberly, "I know that. That doesn't make murder right, does it?"

"No," Justice answered. "It doesn't. Go on, get your horse. I'll wait for you."

Together then they rode out of Hardship, toward the mountains to the east. Thunder crackled distantly. Those clouds still hadn't made up their mind what they were going to do, but there was the smell of sulfur in the air . . . sulfur and something else, less definable, almost like the scent of trouble, if there is such a thing.

"I didn't know you were in town, Mister Justice. Neither did Dirk. We just went to the livery to get a shoe tacked down. The roan threw one along the trail."

"But so long as I was there, he decided to kill me."

"Something like that." Sandy grinned. "He didn't really want to kill you, you know. I've never seen him go at anyone with a gun before—he must have been scared of you. But he's a bully, yes. He wants to dominate this small corner of the world, his corner, with fists."

"To dominate your old man?"

"Nobody dominates him," the kid answered seriously. "Not King Forrest. He's crippled up now, but you should have seen him when I was growing up. We drove those cattle we have all the way from south Texas. And there was a lot of fighting—Comanche arrows are what did that to my father. Anyway, he doesn't quit, he won't quit until he gets what he wants. Dirk knows that. Dirk's been with Dad for twenty years."

"A long time to work for wages." They had to stop talking as they forded a quick-running stream where huge boulders littered the bottom and the hiss and swirl of water overpowered their voices.

On the far side, as they went into the silent forest again, Sandy said, "If you think Dirk would cross Father, you're wrong. My father *is* a king to him. Dirk is one of those feudal ranch hands—all for the brand, for the owner. You've met them if you've been down in Texas. They'd die for the brand."

"You speak as if you see your father as a king too, Sandy."

"He's my father, that's all," Sandy said enigmatically. He changed the subject. "Natalie is fine. She doesn't know what happened this morning. The knife, I mean—I found it."

"She doesn't *know* what happened?" Ruff asked with disbelief.

"No . . ." Sandy fell silent after starting to say something else. "What are you going to do now?"

"Find a girl named Sue Blackcastle. I don't suppose you've heard of her."

"No." Sandy shook his head. "I never have heard the name. Is it tied in with the Morgan horse or the claim to your brother's ranch. The murder?"

"I wish I knew, Sandy. I swear to you, I don't even know that, but I mean to find out."

"Then I'll go with you."

"Why?" Ruff Justice pulled the little gray up and sat facing Sandy Forrest. "Why would you want to get involved in this? Is your family involved? Are you riding herd on me for your father?"

"Not for him."

"Then what?"

"Didn't you know?" Sandy asked. "The day your brother was killed—there was a witness, an old Indian. There was a man at the cabin the day Roland Justice died. And there was a woman. It was the woman that killed him."

9

Ruff Justice sat the gray and watched the kid's eyes.
The wind was working in the pines, groaning and
shrieking. "What's all of this, Sandy? A woman killed
my brother?"

"Yes."

"And there was a witness to it?"

"Only an old Indian. His name was Packrat."

"I want to talk to him."

"He's gone."

"How gone?" Ruff demanded.

"Like you'd think. Dead. Someone found him
murdered. It wasn't much looked into. We got no
law, and anyway it was just an Indian."

"He saw the murder?"

"Not exactly. He was telling the story around for
whiskey. Sometimes he would say he'd seen the
woman, like a ghost woman all in white, near naked.
Sometimes she'd be blond, sometimes very dark.
Sometimes he didn't know what he'd seen, but he
swears he was there and saw the murderers. A man
and a woman."

"And somebody believed him."

"Yes," Sandy said. "Someone believed him, because they found Packrat dead."

"A woman . . ."

"Now, wait a minute," Sandy said, "don't you get to thinking—"

"Thinking what?"

"Nothing."

But Ruff already had the image of the woman who had slashed at him with a knife that morning in his mind. The dark-eyed, beautiful woman, named Natalie Forrest.

"You're wrong if you think that," Sandy said.

"I told you I wasn't thinking anything. I'm just turning it over in my mind. I've got too many questions, too few answers. Just now I want to find Miss Sue Blackcastle and her father."

"You don't mean the folks in that high, enclosed wagon?" Sandy asked.

"Don't I?"

"Well, I mean—you said the name 'Blackcastle' and that didn't mean a thing. But I've seen that girl and her father. Salty thing she is, too."

"Where?"

"On our property. Or near enough. It could be your brother's land . . . nobody seems to know how the title settled. But anyway, they're up there. Not far from your brother's cabin."

"And the tattooed man?"

"I don't know what you mean. What tattooed man?"

"Never mind. Show me where that wagon is."

"I'm riding with you, then?"

"For now."

Sandy grinned. "Good. I reckon I'll show them something. I'll show my father that I can do without him."

Ruff frowned. What was eating the kid exactly? Overshadowed by a domineering father, he had some sort of identity problem working at him. Just now the scout didn't have time to worry about the kid's personal problems. "Show me where the Blackcastle wagon is parked," he said.

They rode south around a tall granite knob called

the Ute's Thumb, winding down through a pretty little cedar-rife valley. Ruff was looking at the knob of stone. Sandy Forrest saw him turn in his saddle and stare back, frowning.

"What do you see?" Sandy asked.

"Nothing, I don't suppose."

"I was afraid it was Utes maybe."

"They've been up this far?" Ruff asked.

"Not for years, but everyone expects them to come back. Half Moon wants to drive us out of these mountains. There it is."

Sitting beside a quickly flowing stream was a tall enclosed wagon, painted black and dull green. Sitting beside it was an old man with white whiskers and a bandanna tied around his head. All that was missing was the peg leg. Ruff would have bet Blackcastle, if that was who it was, had spent more years walking a rolling deck than he had on dry land.

"Going on down?" Sandy asked.

"Yeah." Again Ruff was thinking of something far away, and Sandy couldn't figure out what it was. He just sat his gray, twirling that new branding iron he'd gotten from the smith. "Let's go on down—if you're still with me?"

"I'm with you."

"What about your dad?"

"What do you mean?"

"He wants my hide, Sandy, and you know it. I've got one reason for being in these mountains: I want to find the one who killed my brother. You say it was a woman. Well, maybe, but there's no way of proving that now. What if my trail leads close to your home, Sandy?"

"What do you mean?"

"Flat out? What if it was your father or your sister that killed Roland? What if it was Dirk or someone else working for your father?"

"It wasn't," the kid answered positively. "You think it was Natalie, but it wasn't. You check on it, Ruff

Justice, and you'll find out she was with me *and* my father at Bear Creek seventy miles from here the morning your brother was killed. That can be verified."

"All right. By who? What's in Bear Creek anyway?"

"Nothing is there. Old Hodge Perkins had a little cabin. The Utes got him. We had a little funeral for him. We were there, like I said, and a half dozen others. Want the names?"

"Yes," Ruff said, "later."

They splashed across the creek. The gray balked a little, but Ruff put him straight and they rode into the camp of the sailor man.

The girl came to the door of the wagon, which was roughly painted, resembling a gypsy's wagon more than anything but without the color and gilt.

The old man never rose from his chair as Ruff swung down and walked toward him. "Mister Black-castle?"

"Ruffin T. Justice?"

The girl slammed the door to the wagon, disappearing inside. "She doesn't like me, I guess," Ruff said.

"The child's got no manners," Blackcastle said. "My fault—I left her to grow up alone. I was sailing, always a sailing man. I guess you kenned that."

"I did." Ruff crouched down beside the old man, plucking at the grass at his feet. "This is Sandy Forrest, by the way."

"And what kind of critter do you call that thing?" Blackcastle asked, meaning the dog, which had seated itself by Ruff.

"Where's the tattooed man?" Ruff asked outright.

"Santos?"

"Is that his name?"

"Yes, Santos. He's not here. Why would he be here? Him and me are blood enemies, don't you know that? I'd shoot the bastard on sight."

"Is that so?" Ruff asked. "Your daughter and you were seen with him in town."

"Maybe to nod at, I seen him, but he's no friend of mine." The sailor spat. "What say we get down to business, Mister Ruffin T. Justice. Where's the damned treasure got to?"

"I thought you said treasure."

"You're damned right I said treasure." The sailor stoked up his pipe, blowing smoke through his wreath of white whiskers.

"I haven't got an idea in the world what you're talking about," Justice said.

"Come on now, son." The sailor winked and leaned forward. "You're Roland's brother. He must have told you. Maybe he sent you a map?"

"He never sent me a thing I can recall. And I haven't talked to him for over ten years. It was nothing personal—he just wasn't there."

"Can't you send that dog off?" Blackcastle said with sudden irritation. "Tell him to go chase squirrels."

"I can't make him do anything much," Ruff said. "Don't like no animal bigger than I am."

"When's Santos coming back?"

"Why . . ." Blackcastle smiled, showing yellow teeth. "Didn't I tell you we weren't mates, him and me?"

"You told me. Now I want you to tell me something else. What's this treasure, Blackcastle?"

"Amos will do. You can call me Amos. I'm a friendly man."

They heard the wagon door slam again, saw the girl leap down and run for the forest. The dog bounded after her.

"No manners, like I said," Amos Blackcastle grumbled. "I sent her on up to the cabin the other day, don't blame the girl for that. I thought there might be something in there."

"Hasn't Santos already been through it? He's been here a long time, from what they tell me, hanging around—looking for treasure?"

" 'Course he's looking for it, Ruffin T. Justice. 'Course! Santos is no fool. As for him being here long, I wouldn't know."

"He has been. Maybe since my brother was killed. I know it's been months he's been skulking around these hills."

"You know a lot, don't you, Mister Justice?"

"Just about half of everything, it seems." Ruff stood. "Why don't you fill me in on what I don't know?"

"What about the kid?" Blackcastle lifted his chin toward Sandy Forrest. "What's his tack?"

"He's with me for now."

"I don't give no shares."

"Shares to what? You don't have the treasure, do you?"

"No." Blackcastle chuckled. "There's that. All right, have it your way. What's our deal if we find it?"

"I didn't come up here looking for treasure. I don't much believe there is any treasure."

"Ah, that's where you're wrong, Ruffin T. Justice. Sue, stop that running!" The girl was racing the dog across the meadow. She ignored her father completely. "The treasure, yes, it's here. It has to be. Roland Justice had it. He stole it from under our noses.

"The ship was Santos'," the old sailor continued. "She was a quick little barkentine and we worked the African coast, doing some blackbirding, some ivory trading. We ran smack into that Arab trader at Takoradi on the Gold Coast. There she was with her main mast snapped, stuck in harbor while they overhauled it, and there we were with our three little four-inch guns. Well, it was fate. Santos said so and we agreed.

"We put two across her bow to let her know we meant business and then we went aboard. Gold! You never saw such a weight of gold in your life, all kinds of baubles and jewelry—silks and such, too, which we left behind.

" 'Boys,' Santos said, 'we've struck it. If we can

make the States without getting hailed by some man-o'-war, I'm giving it up. There's nothing left to sail for. We're set for life.'

"Well, we made it back. Calm waters, fresh winds all the way. Then we put in to that Mexican port and got a little liquored up. When we came around, me and Santos and Black Jack, the ship was gone. Plain gone. Your brother, the Mexicans said, was the man in command."

"And then what?" Ruff asked. He didn't quite buy the story, not the way Blackcastle told it. Roland a pirate? Maybe, but Justice couldn't believe he'd steal from his own kind. Not without cause.

"And then what happened?" Ruff repeated.

"I don't know. That's all of it. It was two years later when Santos said he'd found Roland in Colorado. Told me to stay off his trail, though. Threatened me, did Santos."

Sandy Forrest asked, "You mean Roland Justice brought all that gold and what-not you were talking about all the way to Colorado? Up into these mountains?"

"I don't know. I don't know what he did with it. Maybe it's in some eastern bank. Maybe he drank it all away or gave it to a Tibetan princess. All I know is, he had it."

Sandy shook his head. "If I had that gold, I wouldn't be living in these lonely mountains."

"Aye, but Roland Justice was a different sort. He always talked about the mountains he'd seen once. That was what got Santos onto his trail finally."

"And you followed Santos," Ruff Justice said.

"That's it."

The girl was walking toward them, swinging a stick. Her breasts rose and fell with the exertion. The dog was at her side. "Well?" she demanded. "Did he come through, Pop?"

"We haven't got around to that point yet, Sue," the sailor said.

Ruff stood up, dusting his hands together. "Yes we have. We got to it and went right on by, Blackcastle. I don't know where Roland put it, if it exists or ever did. I couldn't even make a decent guess."

"No," Sue said, rolling up her yellow hair to pin it at the base of her skull. She spoke around a hairpin in her mouth. "If he knew where it was, don't you reckon he'd be off getting it, Pop?"

Blackcastle sighed and admitted reluctantly that she was right. "Still—a man has hopes." He waved a hand around him at the vastness of the wilderness. "If it's up here, how the hell's anyone going to find it, ever?"

There wasn't any answer to that question. An idea was slowly beginning to work in Ruff's mind, but he would have to give it a lot of study before he could give it much weight. Still, it was possible.

"Get out of here."

The voice cut sharply across the momentary silence. The rushing river had covered the sound of his approaching footsteps. Sue Blackcastle continued to pin her hair up, her expression not changing a bit.

Ruff turned slowly to find the tattooed man behind him. There were no tattoos visible except at the base of his throat where his shirt was open. He wore yellow kid gloves over his hands. He had a sharp, dark face with concave cheeks. The eyes were narrow and dark, a seaman's eyes. Rays of weather-cut lines fanned out from the corners of his eyes. He wore blue jeans and a red cotton shirt. He also had a Colt revolver on his hip, and seaman or nor, Justice would have bet Santos knew how to use it.

"Mister Justice was just going," Blackcastle said with a little chuckle.

"You stay away from here," Santos said, taking a step nearer. The dog growled deep in its throat, but Santos didn't even glance that way. "It's my treasure, you hear?" he said. "My treasure, and that's my woman there."

Sue broke into laughter and Santos' scowl deepened. The old man was rocking away in his chair. Ruff nodded to Sandy Forrest. "Let's light out." He'd already had one brawl, and that was his usual limit for the morning.

"He doesn't want your gold," Sandy said, and there was some starch in his voice. "He just wants the one who killed his brother."

"Take the whelp away," Santos said with a contemptuous wave of his hand. Sandy stiffened but held himself back. It was good that he had, Justice thought. Santos had been around the world, and he had made bloody tracks. He was a buccaneer and a killer. A man just a little out of Sandy Forrest's league.

"Good-bye, Ruffin," Sue cooed at him as he swung up. She came to his horse and rested a hand on his knee. "You come back some time, or maybe I'll be up to see you." Santos was stiff with anger. Sue Blackcastle was playing a very dangerous game.

Her hand slowly slid away, and she stood, hands on hips, watching as Ruff turned his gray and rode off, the dog following, Sandy Forest coming last.

It was already growing dark when they rode past the Ute's Thumb again and they halted at the fork in the trail.

"I've got to get on back to the ranch. I guess I'm in deep trouble anyway, if anyone saw me with you."

"Stay out of it completely, kid. It's not worth it."

"Maybe not. Maybe I'd like to find out who did the killing too, Mister Justice. I'd like the cloud lifted from my family's heads."

"I can understand that, but there's too much going on. I'm not sure I understand it all myself. There are too many people with guns and grudges wandering around in the hills. You keep your head low—a little good advice."

"If you need me," Sandy said, "you know where I

am." Then Ruff turned and rode off through the gathering dusk toward Roland's cabin.

It wasn't much of a homecoming.

They had come and dug up the grave. Sod was strewn everywhere. The shovel, apparently one of Roland's own, was thrust at a strange angle into a pile of dark earth. They'd gone down a good six feet before giving it up.

And beside the open grave was Natalie Forrest.

10

She haunted the place, this sad, dark ghost of a woman. As Ruff came up to her, she turned her head slowly toward him.

"They didn't have to do this," she said.

"They thought the treasure was there."

"Yes." She shrugged. The notion of a treasure didn't seem to surprise her any. Maybe Roland had told her. Of them all it seemed to be Natalie that he was close to, cared about.

She seemed different today, subdued. He wondered if she still had that little knife concealed about her person.

"You don't know who did this?" Ruff asked. Not that it was very important.

Natalie bent to pick up a crushed mountain lilac. "I just brought these today . . . I saw a man in a red shirt as I rode up. That's all I know."

"Santos."

The woman only shrugged. The flower dropped from her hand and she stood blank-eyed staring at the sunset skies, all orange and deep blue above the far mountains.

"It's getting cold. I've got to see to my horse. Go on in if you want. You'll find coffee."

She didn't respond. Ruff walked away, taking up

the gray's reins. He rubbed it down and left it in the little lean-to stable Roland had built behind the house. The hay was not the best, dark with age as it was, but the horse didn't seem to mind.

"I'll cut you some fresh tomorrow," Ruff said. He tossed his saddle over the sawhorse placed there for that purpose, turned, and went out.

The skies were deep purple. The thunderheads were again bulging southward, blocking out the stars. The highest cloud was touched with fading pink. Ruff looked toward the grave. She was gone.

"Come on," he told the dog, "I'll find you something to eat."

It trotted along behind him through the dusk. Ruff smelled the coffee boiling before he had opened the front door. He smiled to himself and went in. Natalie was there, looking relaxed yet distant, sitting in the rocker near the fire as Sue Blackcastle had.

"I decided to stay for a minute or two. I'm not putting you out?"

"No." Ruff took off his hat and wiped back his long dark hair.

Natalie was watching him. "It is amazing, you know. The resemblance."

"Are you hungry?" he asked. "Dog and I need something to eat."

"No. Please go ahead."

Ruff opened up three tins of beef—one for himself, two for the dog. He had that and coffee for supper. Natalie sat staring at the fire as if she had been transported to another world.

He couldn't figure her at all. Hadn't she tried to wipe a knife across his belly that morning? She seemed so peaceful, so distant from violence that it was hard to believe . . . unless she were truly mad. And then what? Had Roland loved her as she apparently had loved him? Or had she killed him?

A woman had done it, the old Indian said. Until someone had killed the old Indian. Sandy had told

Ruff that the Forrest family had been over the hills in Bear Creek . . . unless that was just a tale.

"The day it happened," Ruff said, "do you remember where you were that day, Natalie?"

"Yes." Her head never turned toward him. She stared at the flames. "Irony. Yes, I recall. I was at Hodge Perkins' funeral in Bear Creek."

That proved nothing either way, but Ruff believed her. Dammit, he believed her.

The fire was burning low. Outside, the wind was blowing hard. He heard the patter of raindrops on the sod roof, and he stepped to the doorway to see the storm coming in, opening up.

"Hard weather. You'd best get started for home."

"It's too far," Natalie said. "I'd be drenched."

"You can't stay here."

"Sure I can." She smiled and Ruff felt a stirring in his groin, felt his heart lift a little. She was there and beautiful, warm by the fire, dark-eyed and sensuous. Or was that all illusion? If it was, it was the best-laid snare Ruff had ever run up against. He walked to her and stood, his hand on the back of the rocker, watching the fire. Her hand lifted from her lap and went across her shoulder to rest on his.

He stood there that way for a long time, watching the embers burn to ash, listening to the rain on the roof. She turned her eyes to him at last.

"I can't go home."

"All right. I'm not going to make you," Ruff said.

She stood then, and with one hand she began unbuttoning the front of her dress. Her right hand was unpinning her sleek dark hair, which tumbled free as her left finished with the buttons.

She stepped from her dress, saying nothing. Ruff watched, walking to the door to drop the bar across it. She was difficult to figure, but she was desirable, there was no doubt about that.

As he turned back, he found her there naked, fire-glossed, her thighs smooth and tapered, breasts jutting, dark-nippled, waist concave and small. Her eyes glistened. Her hands reached out toward Justice, her fingers wiggling impatiently.

Ruff started that way. The light in the room was golden; shifting shadows painted the walls, danced across her nude body. Ruff was in front of her now and she looked up at him once and then began undoing his belt.

Her hands were trembling a little. Ruff's lips dropped to her shoulder, to the smoothness of her neck. She gave a little puff of frustration and Justice helped her with his pants, helped her slip her hands inside where they brushed his growing erection and cupped his sack.

She sagged against him for a minute, unmoving; then she began tugging at his shirt. In another moment it was up over Ruff's head and she was walking him backward toward the bed.

Ruff sat down on the edge of it and Natalie sank to her knees. He kissed the top of her head, liking the scent of her newly washed hair. His hands reached down and filled themselves with her warm, firm breasts. She sighed, kissing his arm before she leaned back and began tugging at his boots.

She was humming softly now. Outside, it was raining to beat the band; inside, all was warm and soft.

She tugged at his pants and they came off and she remained there, kneeling, her eyes wide and deep. Her hands roamed over his maleness, toying with the head of his shaft, until she gave a little quiver and her head sagged forward, her hair draping itself across his lap as her lips crept across his inner thighs.

Ruff lay back and she came to him, straddling him. He could see her face in the golden glow of the firelight, intent, beautiful; he saw the marvelous young breasts, which called his hands and his lips to them.

He felt her shift, lift her leg across him, and then clutch at his erection, holding it with both hands, feeling the slow throbbing of it. Then slowly she touched it to herself, to the warm inner flesh that waited for him.

With a quick little movement and a tiny gasp she lowered herself onto Ruff Justice, who was on his back, stroking her breasts, abdomen, thighs, watching her face, seeing the pleasure written there as she worked herself against him, swaying forward and back, lifting herself a bare inch at a time, slowly settling again with a deep trembling. She reached behind her ass and found Ruff's sack and she held it, pressing it against her soft, damp cleft.

Natalie gave a sudden little jerk and then she lay forward, her breasts grazing Ruff's lips as she worked backward and forward, her breath coming tightly.

She touched Ruff's shaft, touched herself where he entered her, and she moaned a little as she leaned forward again, her mouth locking onto his, soft, pliant, searching. Her body began a furious race toward completion, and Justice, feeling the sudden rush of dampness with her and hearing her soft, needful encouragement in his ear, began to arch his back, to drive it in deeper yet, to bury himself in her as she sat upright, her eyes distant, almost stunned, before with a quaking last exertion she found her sudden climax. Ruff dragged her head down to him, kissed her mouth bruisingly, and his own body released its completion.

She lay there, breathing softly, her heart thumping against his. His hands caressed her buttocks, the small of her back, her shoulders, and she dozed there, satisfied, small, complete.

And only once in all that time did she call him Roland.

She was gone in the morning. How she had done that was a mystery to Ruff. It wasn't that easy for people to move about while he was sleeping. Ruff had his own alert system, something purely unconscious, sometimes eerie, which caused his body to come alert when people started tippy-toeing around.

She had not only gotten up, but dressed and gone out.

"You're a big help, too," Ruff said to the dog, which, head on paws, looked up with yellow eyes.

The funny thing was that the dog also trusted her. With a start, Ruff realized it was true; he *did* trust Natalie. Why he should have, he didn't know. If there was a suspect for the killing, she was it. She had tried to cut him the other morning ... Why, then?

He couldn't answer the question, but trust her he did.

She was damned near the only one in those mountains he did trust.

He thought things over again as he made coffee and got dressed himself, the newly stoked fire burning brightly. Blackcastle and Santos. Hardly trustworthy, but why would they kill Roland before they had gotten the treasure or a map to it? Not likely, but then Santos seemed to be a man of passion. Ruff recalled his explosion when Sue had paid a little attention to him.

"Killed Roland in a huff, maybe. Regrets it now but can't do anything to change matters."

Maybe.

Forrest and his crew were still the prime suspects. Forrest and his children might have been at the funeral in Bear Creek when Roland was shot, but what about John Dirk and the gunman? Killed for a horse? Sure—a hundred-thousand-dollar horse. Men have been killed for two dollars.

Ruff fed the dog again—with his last tin of beef. He was going to have to go hunting or rustle one of Forrest's steers. He smiled thinly at that thought.

Opening the door to the cabin, Ruff was met by a cold, twisting blast of wind. Outside, it was still coming down, a hard slanting rain. It was like peering through steel mesh to look out across the valley, toward the desecrated grave. He closed the door and had another cup of coffee by the fire.

He wanted two things: the Morgan horse and Roland's killer. There was no telling if the matters were connected. The horse was long gone, no one knew where. The killer, Ruff had at first thought, was one of a few people. Now his list seemed to go on endlessly from Forrest through Dirk and the dark-eyed gunman, to Santos and Blackcastle, the two women. . . .

"Is there a treasure?" he asked himself. Santos seemed to think so. "All right, if there is, is there something else? Something to indicate who might have wanted Roland dead badly enough to do the deed? Maybe."

Maybe. Ruff looked to the table where he had the branding iron he had gotten in town. The branding iron Roland had designed himself. It seemed unnecessarily ornate. The "RJ" twisting around with many curlicues and twists in a way that had reminded Ruff of a seaman's knot. Now it made him think of something else. He had first noticed it yesterday as he and Sandy rode slowly back to the mountains from Stokes' store.

Ruff thrust the iron into the fire and sat watching thoughtfully while it warmed and then glowed a cherry red. He walked with it to the wall when it was hot, and choosing a smooth surface on the logs, he touched the iron to it. There was a small hiss, the faint odor of burned wood. Ruff put the iron aside and stood looking at the wall, nodding. He had spent most of his time looking at that iron backwards. Now it was the way it would appear on stock, and if Ruff was wrong, then he was going crazy, because he could make it all out.

"Damn you, you conniving bastard," Ruff said in fond memory of Roland Justice.

It was the iron. If you looked long enough, if you knew where you were starting, the black iron formed a map. At the cap of the "R" there was a small loop. That was the cabin. You knew that because of the other flange, which represented the high ridge. It was all there, plain as day. Ruff had first seen it when he had been sitting his horse, watching the river wind past Ute's Thumb. The knob of rock, the line of the river had touched some very recent memory, but he hadn't been able to quite put his finger on it.

Now he thought he had.

"You devious bastard," Ruff said again in admiration. How long it must have taken Roland to figure this one out was beyond him. The smith had had his work cut out for him, but he had done it properly. It was very nearly to scale, Ruff thought.

And down at the bottom where a last little flourish was formed by the iron-maker's skill there was a point where two lines crossed. And if you were looking just right, if you had enough imagination, it was very much like an "X" marked on a map.

He hadn't replaced the bar when he closed the door this last time, and in a moment he regretted it. He heard the approaching feet, the crash, but by the time Ruff could reach for his gun they were already there in the doorway, rifles leveled.

The dog leapt at their throats, and Santos' rifle cracked. The dog flopped down on its side, whimpering for a minute, then lying still. There was a red smear on his skull.

"Dammit, you didn't have to do that," Sue Blackcastle said, pushing forward.

"The hell I didn't. He would have bitten my face off. You hold steady there, Justice. Amos, get around there and lift his guns."

The old man moved warily around the table, coming up behind Justice, relieving him of the weight of his Colt. The girl was still on the floor beside the big gray dog.

"How is he?" Ruff asked.

"Aw, I don't know. He's been creased on the skull. Sometimes . . . Why'd you shoot him, Santos?"

Santos didn't answer. All three of the intruders had rainslickers on. Outside, it was still pouring. They could hear it drumming down on the roof.

"What is this?" Ruff asked. "A little murder party?"

"Not unless you turn it into one," Santos said. He had no gloves on now, and Ruff could see the purple and red lines snaking across his flesh in demonic profusion. What was it that caused a man to cover himself all over like that? A little touch of madness, surely.

"We're going treasure hunting, and you're going with us," Amos Blackcastle said.

"We are? Where are we hunting exactly?" Ruff asked. "Come across a map, did you?"

"No, did you?" Santos asked, his eyes narrowing.

"Santos, says—and damn me if I'm not convinced— that there'd be only one reason for you comin' all this way, and that's to find that treasure," Amos Blackcastle said.

"Santos is wrong. You're wrong."

"Shut up," Santos said. He was poking around, digging through Ruff's things, tossing the mattress off the bed.

"Santos says your brother couldn't have been that negligent. Somebody has to know where the treasure is. A man don't go out without letting someone know."

"If he doesn't know he's going out . . ."

"You're going out if you don't button your lip and give us some help." Santos countered. "He told the girl anyway."

"He what?"

"He told the girl there was a map," Santos said. "Didn't he, Sue? What do you think I've been wasting my time around here for? I knew there was a map."

"Why would he tell her?"

"She knew the right question and when to ask it,"

Amos said with a snigger. Santos didn't like that
answer. Maybe he really did have a thing for Sue
Blackcastle.

"He told her, all right. Since he died, we've been
looking for it. I can show you every hollow tree in a
hundred miles. I was out of inspiration until you
showed up, Ruffin T. Justice. Then it hit me."

"It should've hit you harder. Knock some of this
nonsense out of your head."

"You're a joker, aren't you, Justice? Just like your
brother. You find too many things funny. Well, this
ain't funny. That's my treasure, and I want it. The
map's not here—that means you got it."

"Or there wasn't one."

"Sue says there was."

She was still beside the dog, which lay still, flanks
quivering. Santos bellowed, "Get up and leave that
son of a bitch alone. Layin' around with a dead dog."

"He's not dead."

"Want me to fix that?"

"Santos . . ."

"Get up, then," the tattooed man said, and she
rose, her rain slicker rustling. She turned her back to
all of them and stared at the wall, uttering a soprano
oath from time to time.

The door suddenly opened again and Santos
whirled, dropping to a knee, his gun coming up.
The wind drove the rain in and Sandy Forrest, standing there with his eyes wide, thrust his hands toward
the ceiling.

"God's sake, don't shoot!"

"Get inside. Close the door. Anyone with you?"

"No."

"Take a look, Amos."

"Aye, Captain."

"You, Justice, hold still," Santos snarled.

Amos came back in shaking his head. "Can't see
anyone."

"Bar the damned door. You, kid, what are you doing here?"

"Why, I just came over to see Mister Justice."

"You've seen him. For the last time."

"No," Sue said shrilly. "You can't kill him, he knows this country better than any of us anyway."

"What are you all talking about?" Sandy asked with a little stutter.

"We're going treasure hunting."

"I told you I don't have the map," Ruff Justice said.

"I don't believe you—I've told you that."

Ruff said, "You're wasting your time."

"Yes, well, I've wasted plenty at this already. It won't bother me any. I've a notion you know where that gold is hidden. And you either take us to it or it's up with you, get me?"

"Just like it was up with Roland?"

Santos didn't respond to that. "You just lead us to where he hid that treasure. If we don't find it, you'll not be coming back out of the mountains, Justice."

If Ruff went up with Santos, he wasn't counting on coming back at all, one way or the other. The funny thing was that up until a few minutes ago he'd had no idea where the treasure was. Now he thought he knew and he was having trouble convincing Santos otherwise.

"What about the kid?"

"He goes."

"What's the point in that, Santos?"

"He goes. He can scout trail, he can help carry our goods. Besides, I can't leave him behind. He goes or he stays here—there's a grave already dug outside waiting for someone to fill it."

"It'll be all right, Ruff," Sandy said. The kid looked ashen, very scared. Ruff didn't blame him. Water dripped off his slicker onto the floor of the cabin. "I trust Mister Santos. He'll keep his word."

"Sure," Ruff said quietly. "You can always trust a snake. To bite."

Santos stepped to him and backhanded Ruff viciously. Blood filled his mouth. Santos had stepped back. The ratcheting of his pistol's hammer was loud in the following stillness, as menacing as a snake's rattle.

"You shut up," Santos said, and his voice was nearer a hiss than speech. "You just keep your mouth shut. You're alive as long as I think you can help me—maybe. If you start shooting off your mouth, I'll kill you. I swear it."

"There, now," Amos Blackcastle said almost cheerfully. "That's straightened out. Shall we get on the trail while the rain's there to cover our tracks?"

"Sure," Justice said.

Santos was still glowering at him. There was a slight trembling to the tattooed man's hand, and the muscles of his throat worked erratically. He was just a little bit off normal, Ruff thought. But he was right about one thing: before this was over, one of them was going to have to die.

Ruff got his coat and they went out into the cold gray day.

11

They rode in silence up the dark road, Ruff Justice in the lead, Santos behind him with his gun hand inside his rain slicker, cradling his Colt. Amos and Sandy came next, the old man voluble, as cheerful as if it were a picnic, the kid somber and silent. Sue Blackcastle, appearing only irritated, came last, her wide floppy hat shedding water in buckets.

The pines were close around them, dark and rich in scent. The rain was cold and constantly in their faces.

Ruff was leading them to the treasure of the Arab prince. Why not? What was the point now in trying to evade it? Santos was going to kill them anyway—him and Sandy. But maybe there was a slight chance for the kid if they found the gold.

Sooner or later they would find out Ruff was bluffing if he pretended not to know, and he didn't know the country well enough to fake a route anyway. And so he went by the map that had been burned in his mind. It was slow going, the weather swirling around them, dark cottony clouds shutting out the mountains entirely, then gaping wide.

As they rode higher, it got colder, very much colder. Ruff thought it would surely snow that night. He could see the Ute's Thumb now and the high peak called Royale—that was recognizable from the iron. Justice shook his head again in admiration at his brother's ingenuity.

Ingenious, but it hadn't helped him to stay alive. Sometimes brains just don't count.

"I hope you know where you're going," Santos said from behind Ruff.

"I know."

"I'm not kidding about killing you if we don't find that treasure."

"I never thought you were," Ruff Justice answered.

"The kid—what's his game?" the tattooed man wanted to know.

"I don't know. He was going to help me look for Roland's horse, that's all."

"What horse?"

"A big Morgan stallion. It's supposed to be hidden somewhere up here."

"Hidden?" The idea was incomprehensible to Santos, a seafaring man who had no idea of the value of certain horses. "Like the treasure."

"Exactly."

"Your brother, Roland, he was not a trusting man."

"Time's proven him right, hasn't it?"

"Yeah." Santos chuckled.

"Did you kill him?" Ruff asked. He turned his head and looked at the dark man, at his rain-glossed face, the tattooed hands gripping the reins inexpertly, the trees waving behind him.

"No," Santos said at last. "I didn't kill him. I had cause, but I didn't. I would have made him talk first. It would have been slow," the pirate said in a way that chilled Ruff a little. The funny thing was Justice believed him, believed Santos was not the killer, though how he could take the word of a man like Santos was beyond Justice.

It was a woman. But not Natalie—she had been far away at a funeral for an old friend of the family. How many women were in these hills? How many that Roland had known intimately? How many with cause to kill him?

Justice glanced back only once at Sue Blackcastle, and her gaze, meeting his, was steady and challenging.

Thunder began to sound like close cannonade, and lightning raked the sky. They lost the trail; it wound through the pines, and they had to backtrack. Only the sounds of Santos' violent cursing were audible above the rain and wind.

"We're going to have to hold up," Justice said.

"The hell we are," Santos shouted above the roar of the rain.

"I can't see the landmarks. I don't know where I am."

"The kid knows this country. He ought to know where the trail goes."

"Maybe. But he can't see any better than we can."

"God damn this rain."

"You didn't have to come out in it."

Santos didn't answer. He had come out in the storm because their movements would be difficult for any possible following eyes to discern. He hadn't counted on getting lost. They couldn't see past the first rank of pines. They were dark, heavy with water.

"Well?" Sue demanded. "What are we going to do? Sit here?"

"I don't know," Santos snapped back. Behind him the old man chuckled.

"Maybe we can get above it," Sandy said. It was the first time the kid had spoken since the cabin.

"What?" Santos asked scornfully.

"Sure. A lot of times, up this high, you can get above the weather."

Santos looked to the skies. "Not above this," he decided. His eye had judged many storms and he knew a strong one when he saw it. Ruff tended to agree.

"Let's try again," Justice said. "If we lose the trail, we'll just have to stop for the night."

"At this time of day?"

"You have a better idea?"

"My idea is that I think you know what you're doing, Justice. I think you know where we are exactly."

"Then you're wrong," Ruff said. "I'm newer to these hills than you are. Why don't you find us one of those hollow trees to climb into?"

It wasn't much of a joke. Santos showed his appreciation of it by reaching out and slamming his fist into Ruff's cheek. Justice's head swiveled around. He shook the fog free and sat there looking at the tattooed man.

"That's twice, sailor, twice you've put your hands on me. The third time I'll be down your throat."

"I've got the gun, Justice."

"That won't matter. Do it again and it just won't matter." Ruff Justice said icily. "I'll get to you, and I'll tear your throat out for you."

"You are warning me?" Santos asked with a scratchy laugh.

"Yes. I'm warning you. You'd better listen. There won't be any treasure, will there, if you have to kill me—and I'll see that you have to."

"Why do I believe that you mean this?" Santos asked.

"Maybe because I'm Roland's brother. If you knew him, then you know how we think. There's no such thing as an idle threat. You keep your mouth shut unless you mean every single word you say."

"What's this got to do with gold and finding it?" Amos asked grouchily. "I'm cold and wet; my slicker's got a hole in it. I'm too old to be out traipsing around up here."

"You could have stayed home," Ruff Justice said.

"No, he couldn't," Sue crowed. "Hell, Pa couldn't stay away from this treasure no more than he could quit breathing in and out—it wouldn't be natural."

"Let's get going," Santos said. They rode on, while the rain refused to lift. Ruff had a vague idea where they were, as did Sandy, but none of them could find a landmark to make further travel worthwhile.

"All right," Santos said an hour later, "let's pack it in. Find a place out of the wind."

"We're going to camp out here?" Sue complained.

"We can't find our way back to camp anywhere else," Amos said.

"It's raining!"

Santos looked to the sky. "Well, damn me if it isn't. The lady does have an eye for weather."

"Shut up. Damn the day I ever had a seafaring man for a father."

"That's not right, Sue," Amos Blackcastle said, apparently sincerely hurt.

"Neither is leading your baby girl around in these cold and foggy mountains after some damned treasure that might not even be here," Sue replied, still angry.

"Oh, it's here," the old man said.

"Is it?" Sue was logical. "How the hell could Justice tell you it wasn't if he knew you were going to kill him?"

"Me?" Amos was incensed.

"Santos, then. The pirate king. Tattoo Charlie. What got into you anyway, bringing him around? A man with blue skin—ugh," Sue said, and she made the expression truly one of disgust.

Santos started to grab for the girl, but she turned her horse away, laughing.

"Lay off, Santos," Amos said, surprising Ruff. "I haven't got much, but I do have a daughter and I won't have her harmed."

"She needs a licking."

"Likely, but I'll do it." The two men faced each other, the rain falling between them. "Don't forget, if it comes to it, I've got a gun too, Captain."

"Ah, what are we arguing about?" Santos said, waving an arm. "We're tired, that's all. Tired and cold. Let's find a spot to lay up."

· They found a place. It wasn't the greatest, but it was better than standing out in the force of the storm. Three giant boulders, one as large as a barn, stood together on the slope. Over these a massive pine had blown down, its roots jutting skyward in a tangle. The place was a reasonable shelter for the people. The horses were forced to remain outside, tails to the wind, huddling together.

By the time Ruff, with Santos watching him, had unsaddled the horses and stowed the gear, Amos Blackcastle had started a small fire going. It smoked some, the wood being damp even though he had gotten it from a hollow beneath one of the great boulders. Ruff crouched down next to the fire, his buckskins steaming.

"I don't like this," Sue Blackcastle said, and Ruff looked at her with surprise. It was the first time she had ever displayed any qualms about anything.

"What don't you like?" Santos wanted to know.

"The night. The storm. Looking for this treasure. Who says it's up here?"

"It better be." Santos glanced sharply at Justice. Behind Santos the flames danced eerily across the walls of the boulders, smoky images mingling with the fire-bright reflections. Sue looked downright uncomfortable now. Of course it was cold and the day was far from pleasant, but she looked worried deeply. She had unpinned her blond hair and it hung loosely across her shoulders, drying. Amos was pouring his daughter a cup of coffee.

"There's places where people shouldn't go," Sue went on.

"Yeah. Like to the brig or the Cameroons. Now that's a place—" Amos said.

Sue interrupted him. "Places that belong to other things. Not to living people."

"Oh, God, she's worried about spooks." Santos laughed.

"Well, so what!" she flared up.

"So nothing. Watch out for the boogie man behind you." Santos roared with laughter.

"Nice way to treat me. You're supposed to care for me? Don't make me laugh. I'm not saying anything else. I was better off living at the girls' school even if I did have to scrub all the damn floors."

Santos was still chuckling as he pulled off his jacket and shirt to hang them from the tree roots overhead where the fire could dry them. It was warm enough in the close confines to strip off your shirt. The granite walls of their hideout acted as reflectors for the heat from the fire, and though Santos would smell rather smoky when he dressed again, he'd at least be dry.

"Jesus!" The oath belonged to Sandy Forrest. He was mesmerized by Santos' torso. The pirate was decorated, every inch of him, from fingertips to waist, with blue and red designs. Women in ringlets, dragons, snakes, daggers, sailing vessels, four aces, meaningless curlicues and ornamentation in flourishes of budding roses and vines, flamelike tongues all frozen there like images captured in ice.

Santos looked at the kid, his expression cold and blank, though the pirate must have been used to people gawking by now. Ruff himself was staring into the eyes of a yellow-eyed tiger that lived on Santos' shoulder.

"What makes a man do that?" Sandy said as if he couldn't keep himself from speaking. No one said a word. Santos moved away, sipping his coffee.

"Got another cup?" Ruff Justice asked. "Mine's with my gear in the cabin."

"Sure," Sue Blackcastle said. She got it for Ruff, pouring it for him and then easing up next to him to crouch too closely beside him as he sipped it. Santos watched with angry eyes.

"Do you think the dog will live?" the girl asked Ruff.

"I don't know. You kind of like him, don't you?"

"Yeah. Did you name him, like I told you?"

"No. You can have the honor."

"Hell, no sense naming him now, if he don't make it."

"He'll make it."

"He'll be frightened. In that cabin all alone—"

"Oh, stow it, Sue," Amos said irritably. "You act like that big snarling beast was a helpless whelp or a baby child."

"It's got feelings, too, I guess," Sue said hotly.

No one answered her. It was nearly the last thing said that night. The fire was fizzling and they were all weary. They rolled up in their damp blankets to pass a miserable night.

They were out with the dawn. That is, if the gray, drizzling morning outside could be called dawn.

The clouds had lifted some and Ruff could pick out his landmarks enough to believe he could find the trail again. He had the map firmly in mind. They were now at the loop of the "R," heading down toward the right-hand leg. That meant straight to the sheer-sided peak ahead of them.

Justice kept his eyes open, waiting for Santos to make a mistake, but the pirate had held prisoners before. Ruff never got behind him, never saw Santos' eyes waver. Amos was always there, too, farther back. Justice didn't know much about the old salt, but he thought he knew enough to understand that Amos would shoot if the "captain" told him to. There were times, when the clouds were thick and the forest deep, that Ruff thought about going for broke, just heeling the gray and taking off, but the chances were always slim. And, anyway, he would be leaving Sandy Forrest behind.

The kid was innocent of everything except wanting to help Justice. Help him find the Morgan stallion and find Roland's killer.

They rode higher now. The trail they followed

twisted and turned, but it was heading for the high peak. Ruff's guesses about the map had all been right, it seemed. Roland couldn't have made it too complicated or no one would ever find that gold.

And the gold had to be there, didn't it? Gold and jewelry, a prince's ransom. It had to be there or Roland wouldn't have made that map.

That afternoon it began to snow.

It drifted down softly, at first mixed with the cold rain they had been having. Then, as darkness began to approach them and they rode higher, the world growing colder, it began to come in seriously, sheeting down to frost their shoulders, the horses, their hats. Ruff's eyelashes and mustache had ice on them. Sue was suffering the most. Sue and the old man. It wasn't so bad in the trees, but at the occasional clearing the driving wind lashed at them, cutting through their clothing.

"Here." Ruff was beside Sue. He slipped his blanket over her shoulders.

She looked at him gratefully. "Thank you."

"It's not much, I'm afraid."

"More than anyone else offered. Ruff, if this keeps up, it's bad for us, isn't it? We're not really prepared for it, I mean."

"No one is prepared for this kind of weather up here," Justice said, shouting above the wind. "Not unless you've got a cabin and a ton of firewood. If this settles in, we might get twenty feet in the passes. It could snow for a week."

"Quit trying to scare her," Amos growled.

"I'm scared myself," Ruff said. "I've been out in a Rocky Mountain winter before. I was lucky to make it through. So," he added, "will we."

"How far do we have to go?" Santos demanded. "I mean, where the hell are you taking us?"

"Just following the map. How far I don't know for sure. I've never been there. But this isn't my idea, remember, to come out looking with the weather like it was."

"He wants it like this, so he can try to get away," Amos put in.

"Sure," Sue said mockingly. "He wants to freeze to death."

"He wants to lose us up here, then come back alone."

"Mister," Ruff said coldly, "I only want to survive."

They didn't make gold worth dying for as far as Ruff was concerned. He glanced at the sky, had his eyes pummeled by driving snow, and shook his head. He couldn't see his marker anymore and they were starting to lose the trail beneath the snow.

"Better start looking for a place," Justice said. "I can't see."

"We haven't come five miles since morning!"

"No, and we're not going much farther. If we stay out in this, we'll be lucky if we ever go anywhere."

"Where the hell ... ?" Santos looked around angrily.

"I know where we are," Sandy Forrest said. "Or pretty nearly. There might be a place we can get out of the wind, though it's going to be pretty uncomfortable."

"Anyplace, kid."

"There used to be a mine over the hump there and a mile north. It played out. There's a shaft there, timbered up, if it hasn't caved in."

"How we going to find that?" Santos shouted.

"It's that or stay out here," Ruff reminded him. With a truly ornate oath Santos heeled his horse into a canter, riding toward the hump.

Ruff had a notion to try it then, while Santos' temper had let his vigilance slip. He didn't hear the hammer of Amos Blackcastle's shotgun pulled back, but he was somehow aware of it. Glancing back, he saw the sailor, his white beard iced, smiling.

"Let's all stick together, Justice."

They rode on.

Conditions were miserable and still worsening. The sky and the land were merging masses of white and gray. The wind was a shrieking, clawing thing out of the north. Twice great pines blew down in their path from the force of the wind.

They took nearly two hours to go the next mile and locate the mine. They would have all given up the search except Sandy convinced them that it was there; Ruff convinced them that if they didn't find it, they were going to die that night.

They stamped into the shaft, shivering, slapping their arms, their faces wrapped with strips of blankets, with scarves. It was cold and dark and icy in the mine shaft, and outside, the wind wailed, drifting snow past the mouth of the tunnel.

They found ancient rotting timbers farther back in the mine and they dragged them out, starting a fire with numbed fingers. They stood, their teeth chattering, until the fire blazed hotly, melting the ice on the stone walls of the mine, seeming to thaw the blood in their veins, freeing it to flow, to warm the chilled flesh.

No one moved away from the fire for a long while. They stood steaming and sighing, moaning, stamping feet, trying to get warm.

"Damn the gold, damn it and all of this territory," Sue spat. She flung her hat away and her hair tumbled free, damp and tangled.

"Now, Sue."

"Now, Sue hell, Pa! What do you want to drag me around up here for?"

"You know, girl, I'm doing this for you, so you can have a decent life." Amos sounded almost sincere.

"A decent life, dead?" Sue mocked. "Do you know what I want? I don't care so much for fancy things I've never had before. What I want is to go down and get truly warm, take a bath, fill my belly with meat and potatoes . . . and sleep!"

"Sue, you know . . ."

"I don't know a thing except that you and Santos are about to drive me crazy," she went on aggressively. "You know you're making us all into outlaws, don't you? Don't look at me like that. You kidnapped these two at gunpoint, didn't you? What else have you done, Pa?"

"I had nothing to do with *that*, if that's what you mean."

"It's what I mean. Roland Justice."

"I didn't do it."

"You could have, you might have. Damn, Pa, I don't want to die up here." She softened her approach, touching the old man's arm. "Can't we wait until the snow stops and then go on back to Hardship? We've got our little wagon there—"

"No one's going," Santos said.

"What do you care?" she asked angrily.

"No one's leaving. Maybe you will shoot off your mouths, huh? Maybe there'll be fifty men after my treasure, then."

"Not unless there's fifty crazy men in Hardship." She waved a hand. "Look out there! It's a blizzard!"

"It'll let up," Santos said.

"And if it doesn't?" Sue demanded.

"Then we go on anyway."

"If it kills us all!"

"We go on," Santos said, his eyes softly gleaming in the firelight. "We go on and we find that gold. No matter what."

12

They all lay down in their bedrolls on the cold stone floor of the abandoned mine shaft. Ice melt trickled down from the walls of the mine as the fire blazed away. Outside, the wind continued to howl, the snow to fall.

If anyone actually slept, no one was much rested from it. They rolled out bleary-eyed, stiff, tired, hungry. They ate dry biscuits and drank coffee.

"It's letting up," Santos said hopefully, nodding toward the mouth of the shaft.

It seemed to be, in fact. Ruff walked that way with his tin cup in his hand, Santos not far behind him. Peering out, he found that he could once more see the sheer-sided peak, very near now, and the vague form of his next landmark, higher up into the mountains.

"All right. It is over. Hurry up and finish the breakfast," Santos shouted. "We're going while there's time."

"Downslope?" Sue asked.

"Downslope, hell. Into the mountains."

The horses were saddled and in half an hour they trailed out through the deep new snow. At noon they found the trail that ran up along the side of the nearly denuded mountain leading toward the next marker, and they turned off, riding higher. They were getting close now, very close, Justice knew. How he was going to find the exact spot he didn't know, but Roland would have made certain there was some kind of indicator.

They were above ten thousand feet now and the wind was bitterly cold. The land was raw, uptilted, slope-sided, empty canyons falling away to gray depths where clouds sometimes swirled. Snow and ice filled the crevices. Otherwise, the wind swept it away from the bare rock underneath. They crossed through a dead forest—miles of trees, all blown down, gray and weathered now, lifeless, a pile of giant's jackstraws.

"Which way now?" Santos shouted as they halted to rest the horses on a high, icy ledge that overhung a mile-deep canyon with landslide-littered slopes. A distant, wildly racing river rushed through the bottom of the gorge.

"The little knob," Ruff said, the wind snatching the words from his mouth as he gasped for breath. A handful of snow, lifted by the wailing wind, stung his cheeks. Ruff pointed ahead still higher up, near the timberline where nothing lived, where nothing could live. A small, nearly round basaltic knob dark against the surrounding granite showed distinctly.

"You're sure?"

"Hell, Santos, I'm not *sure* of any of this," Ruff told him. "That's my best guess, that's all."

"If this is a trick . . ."

"Sure. I'm dying up here so I can trick you. Let's keep moving. This is no place to stop."

They hadn't gone far before they found the Indian tracks.

"Half Moon," Sandy Forrest said fearfully.

"Who's that?" Santos asked.

Sandy explained while Ruff studied the tracks, which ran up a narrow draw toward higher ground. Maybe thirty men, their moccasin tracks clear in the new snow where the wind had not disturbed it.

"How do we know this is Half Moon's bunch?"

"I can't think of any reason for any other Ute band to come up this high, not in this weather. Can you? I'd think it would have to be someone who was running, hiding. Normally the Utes would have drifted south."

"Maybe not," Santos snapped.

"Maybe not," Justice agreed with a shrug.

"There aren't any other Indians around here," Sandy Forrest put in. The kid's eyes were round and frightened. "Only Half Moon. Only the renegade."

"Listen, Santos—" Amos Blackcastle began nervously.

"No, damn you, I'm not listening to anything. Are you going to let a few Indians drive you off course? After the things we've been through? You have any idea what your share of the treasure is worth!"

"Let the girl go back," Amos said.

"We all go together, and we keep going forward."

"Then," Ruff Justice said, "let's get on. The storm's coming in and this is no place to be."

They all looked northward. It was coming in again, all right, clouds like a thundering herd of dark buffalo. They saw lightning arc across the sky from peak to peak, saw an entire forest ruffled by a casual lick of wind.

"We got to get lower," Amos said.

"Justice?"

"I'd agree, but the map says higher yet."

"What map?" Amos demanded fitfully. "How come we've never seen a map!"

"Where, then?" Santos asked. He was watching the northern skies almost dreamily. It was a very bad dream too. When it hit this time, it was coming with all the fury of the elements behind it.

"The trees, if we can make it." Ruff pointed ahead to a thick stand of virgin pine, dark blue against the gray of the pale mountain.

"That's four, five miles on."

"That's right." It was also, Ruff believed, a marker, the final marker. From here the stand of timber seemed to have no shape at all; it was only a smear against the mountainside. But from farther back on the trail it had seemed to form itself into a strange shape. Where the two ridges intersected above the barren valleys below they formed something remarkably like an "X."

It seemed so, and Ruff thought it was, but he couldn't see how that was supposed to point anyone to a treasure. The area covered by the forested ridges was something like ten square miles. Nevertheless, he thought they were going right.

But treasure just now was the least of his worries. They were going to have to survive for anyone to enjoy spending that gold. Right now their chances didn't look that strong to Ruff Justice.

They went on, the wind increasing, buffeting them harshly, whipping coattails and horses' manes. It was cold, so cold that they were reluctant to breathe, and when they did gasp for air, they found little oxygen in it. None of them was used to the altitude.

The trail they were following was little more than a scar against the flank of the pale mountain, and it seemed to go on endlessly, each bend in the road showing them a new one.

Ruff began to get edgy. If they were stuck on the ledge at night, they wouldn't survive. They just wouldn't.

Amos Blackcastle's horse hit the ice, its hooves clattering, its eyes wide with fear, and as Amos bailed out, clutching for the arms of Ruff Justice, for his daughter's hands, the horse went over, cartwheeling through space. It hit rock far, far below, bouncing three times before it disappeared from their sight.

"Jesus, God," Amos breathed. He stood there trembling.

"Get up behind your daughter and let's get going," Santos snarled.

He did, shakily. The party moved on. The skies were darker yet. Lightning flashed continually. The trail, however, began to widen a little, to flatten as it moved toward the trees. It was snowing by the time they had crossed the rocky gorge; snow and great boulders and fallen trees clotted the declivity. Ahead, the patch of trees stood, alone against the miles of barren rock. Some quirk wind kept this spot just warm enough to support life, Justice guessed. Just now the wind was incredibly cold, cutting.

They were into the timber and moving slowly upslope. If there was a trail, no one knew where it was. There was only the forest and the constant snow.

"Where now?" Santos shouted. There was ice on his horse and on his shoulders. He had been riding with a scarf over his face; now he pulled it down to shout again. "Where to?"

"I don't know," Justice said. "I haven't got a clue."

"We can't camp here."

No, they couldn't, and that meant they had serious trouble. It was getting dark, and along with the cold was the chance that they would lose another horse due to a misstep in the dark. All the horses were weakened from the exertion, from the lack of decent graze.

"Look there!" It was Sue who shouted out, standing in her stirrups. "Am I going mad?"

"If you are, I am too," her father said, and they lifted their horses into a staggering gallop. The wind shrieked its mockery and the snow fell, but ahead was the log cabin someone had built in this wilderness.

They swung down before the cabin, weary but cautious.

"Somebody better have a look first," Santos said.

"Give me a gun," Ruff suggested. "I'll look."

"Go to hell, Justice."

Santos, rifle in hand, crept to the front door of the cabin, tracking through the foot-deep snow. He tapped once with the rifle butt and then kicked at the door. It swung in. Santos peered inside.

"All right," he told them. "Come on in. Amos, you and Justice put those horses up."

Sue and Sandy Forrest went along in and Justice took the reins of the horses. Whoever had built the cabin had taken accommodations for horses into account. The cabin abutted a granite face with a natural, time-cut hollow. To that shallow shelter had been added a log shed. Inside, it was dry enough. There was room for all their horses and more.

"Look here," Amos said. "Hay. Where's a man get hay up here?"

"He brought it up himself."

"Your brother."

"That's right."

"Why did he build up here? Why in this godforsaken place?" Amos Blackcastle asked.

"It was his redoubt. His last hideout. He meant to use it when you and Santos showed up, as he knew you would." Ruff was rubbing down the gray vigorously. He wanted that animal in the best shape it could be in. "The forage is for his horses—his Morgan horses. He wouldn't leave them behind—not the stallion, at least."

"Well, you may be right, I don't know. All I know is that I might have cursed Roland Justice for things he done, but I bless his dark heart for this."

"His dark heart?" Ruff stood and faced the old man, who backed away a little, raising his gun. "Who was it that had the black heart, Amos? What really happened?"

"What do you mean?"

"Roland wasn't the man you and Santos describe. He didn't just run off with your gold because he was a blackguard, a thief."

"I tell you he did. Can't you believe anything bad about him? You said yourself you didn't hardly know him. Well, I knew him. I sailed with him three long years."

"All right." There was no profit in that discussion. Ruff pitched hay to the horses and then they stood watching the howl and wash of the storm. "He's going to kill you, you know," Ruff Justice said.

"Santos? Naw, he's the captain. He's going to split with me. Maybe marry Sue . . ."

"And you'll all live together on Sunnybrook Farm."

"I'm tellin' you he wouldn't."

"Why wouldn't he? If word of this leaks out, doesn't the rest of the crew come running? What about this Black Jack I heard you mention, the other mate?"

"Jack won't be coming," Amos said in a muted voice.

"No?"

"Santos had to . . . Black Jack is dead." And now Amos was thinking, which was all Ruff wanted. Let them worry each other just a little. Again he had a notion to try and break loose. He could have taken Amos' gun, he thought. The mate was being most careless. But where would that leave him? Outside, in the blizzard, while Santos had the cabin, the girl, and Sandy Forrest.

"Let's get over there and see if they've got a fire," Ruff Justice said.

They tramped through the snow and falling darkness to the cabin. There was a fire all right when they stepped in. That was all there was. Everyone was gone.

They were gone . . . but they couldn't be! There was no reason for anyone to go out into that blizzard, and besides, Ruff hadn't seen any fresh tracks.

"Son of a bitch," Amos breathed.

"Bar the door behind us."

"Where are they? What's happening?"

Ruff looked at the fireplace, glanced around the cabin, which was ample, bigger than the place Roland had down below. Maybe he had meant to live up here all along, far away from people. But he had stayed down anyway and gotten killed. Why? A woman, maybe. He had stayed because he had fallen for Natalie Forrest. And so they had been able to catch up with him. Now he was dead.

The wall of the cabin was decorated with colored squares, some of one color, others bisected diagonally. Red and yellow, blue and green. Justice frowned.

"What's all this?"

"What?" Amos lifted his eye to the decorations. "International Code. Signal flags the British Board of Trade came up with in '57. They've been trying to get sailing masters to adopt them. Myself I can't see the use of it. Not for a privateer," he added with a short laugh.

"What about Santos? Does he know the code?"

"Sure he does. I know it as well, I just don't . . . Wait a minute. Your brother is telling us something."

"That's right," Ruff said.

Amos went nearer to the wall, looking at the flags. There were 70,000 signals in the book, utilizing eighteen flags, but the common ones a longtime sailor committed to memory.

"Well, it don't make sense," Amos said.

"What is it?"

" 'Open channel starboard,' " Amos replied with a shrug.

Ruff Justice smiled. He turned to his right, walked to the wall, and examined it closely. Seeing the saw marks, he pressed and the wall swiveled in on neatly constructed metal pins.

"Damn me!" Amos said, rushing forward.

The two men looked into the tunnel behind the panel, seeing the firelight around the bend.

"Santos!" Ruff shouted. His cry echoed away.

"Let's go on in," Amos said excitedly.

"I thought it was a good idea to let him know who it was," Ruff replied. "He might be feeling just a little nervous."

"Why? What are you talking about? Oh, God! The treasure! In there?"

"I can't think of another reason Roland would go to this much trouble. Santos? Hear me, we're coming in."

They crept down the corridor, which was another of the mine shafts that dotted these hills. *The* mine shaft, perhaps. The lost gold mine people had been looking for.

They came around the corner of the shaft and found the others frozen into a strange, firelit tableau.

Santos held the torch. Sue Blackcastle was on her knees, her hands digging into the chest, which rested in the nook. Sandy Forrest just gawked. The gold glittered and shone, burnished by the moving torchlight. A chest filled with treasure, pounds and pounds of gold, much of it fantastically wrought jewelry with emeralds and rubies set in it.

Amos made an involuntary little moan and staggered forward. Santos turned slowly toward him, his dark eyes glittering.

"And so. Did you doubt me, Amos? I told you we'd find it."

"I did doubt you. I apologize. I wanted to turn back." Amos crouched and reverently picked up a large crown, turning it in the light.

Ruff Justice spotted something he wanted. "Do you mind?" he asked Santos. The pirate just waved his hand and Justice picked up the black-bound logbook.

"What's that?" Sue asked.

"Roland's diary."

"Help me drag this out," Santos commanded. "Amos, put that crown back."

"No sense taking it out tonight, Captain."

"No sense leaving it in here. I want it where I can see it. As soon as the snow stops, I'm getting out and I'm taking it with me."

Ruff and Amos dragged the chest out, while Santos held the torch and a Colt revolver. How Roland had gotten the thing in there by himself took some imagining. Ruff would have bet that a man with enough time to poke around that tunnel would have come up with some block and tackle. Roland was apparently many things, but no fool.

"Get some coffee boiling, Sue," Santos said. He was flying high.

"When Pop tells me to," she said sharply. "We ain't married."

Santos didn't hear her. He was busy digging through the chest, his eyes as bright as the glittering jewels. "All here, I think. All here," he said, running through a mental inventory.

Ruff Justice sat on an unmade bunk in the corner and opened the diary his brother had left. It began a few days before the mutiny. Ruff skipped over the habitual weather and sea reports and got to the text.

"The captain and mates continue to mistreat the crew members. Regret having signed on this voyage. Santos has been impossible since the Arab trader was taken. Three men flogged to death. I think that he does not want to have to share the hoard."

Ruff glanced at Santos, who was still digging through the treasure. He turned the pages of the diary idly.

"Mexican port tomorrow," Roland had written, "and we are two fewer. A man keelhauled today. Tom Quinn for failing to doff his cap to Santos. We pulled up only chunks of meat. The sharks had been at poor Tom. I swear Santos will not profit by this voyage. Black Jack is nearly as bad as the captain. Amos Blackcastle is an ineffective second mate. As greedy as Santos. I'll take things into my own hands. The crew has balloted secretly and elected me captain. Very well. Then I will do what needs be done."

And two pages on: "Santos is far behind now. The Sea Acts name us all mutineers even if the vessel we sailed was a privateer. We have agreed to split up and not touch the treasure at all for a period of ten years. This is for our own safety. We will scuttle the barkentine and separate. The crew has left it to me to protect the chest for the next decade. By then perhaps Santos will be hanged, as by rights he should be."

The coffee had boiled. Sue handed Ruff a cup and leaned over him. "What's that?"

"A memory," Ruff said, and the girl went away shrugging. Justice read on.

"Built the high cabin and the low one. Still have the Morgan I won at the faro table. Beautiful animal. Will make my living for me." Then "She came and I saw love for the first time in my wretched life. Natalie! Where have you been? If only it weren't for this terrible, deadly cloud that hangs over you . . ."

"What the hell's that?" Santos yanked the book from Ruff's hand, glanced at it, and demanded, "What's he say about me?"

"The truth."

"Damn that man and all that remains of him," Santos said viciously, throwing the diary into the fireplace, where it drew golden sparks. Justice just sat on the bunk, watching the book leaves curl and blacken, knowing that he had just lost the only clue he might have had to Roland's murder.

If only it weren't for this terrible, deadly cloud that hangs over you. . . .

What deadly cloud? A vengeful lover, a protective father, a madness? How else could you explain Natalie's behavior? Was that it, brother? Did you fall in love with a madwoman? Ruff thought sadly. Fall deeply in love and realize only too late what she was, that there was a deep flaw in Natalie Forrest?

Sue was cavorting around with a crown and a gold necklace. Amos had a double handful of gold coins. Santos sat smiling dirtily. Sandy Forrest looked at Ruff and shook his head.

They had a problem now, he and Sandy. They

weren't really needed, were they? The horses could carry the gold—if there were no riders. The mountains could keep a secret better than living men. And what was Santos? A cruel man, according to Roland, according to what Ruff himself had seen.

Yes, he would be wanting to erase the tracks he was leaving. Erase them with death. Outside, the cold wind was still blowing, chanting in the trees, and the words the wind formed were a funeral dirge.

13

····——◆——····

"When?" Amos Blackcastle asked as morning light pierced the cloud cover, glittered on the lightly descending snow.

The pirate captain looked at him. "Let's get everything loaded first. Once we're started back down the trail, anyplace is all right. You take the baby boy. I'm having Ruff Justice for myself."

"You're welcome to him."

Sue came up to them as the two sailors stood just outside the cabin door, watching the apparently clearing weather. " 'Morning," she said happily. "Well, we're all rich."

"And you're the richest," Amos said. He stoked up his stubby pipe.

"Me?"

"Sure, look at you—a rich father and a rich husband, isn't that right, Santos?"

"That's right," the pirate said. He didn't look like he wanted to wait for any preacher, however. Amos was more than a little edgy. There was more killing in the wind—there always was with Santos. Who knew which direction the ax would fall next? He had Sue, of course, and as long as Santos wanted her, Amos was safe as well . . . he hoped. He continued to push her in the captain's direction. Only, sometimes—well, damn her, she had no proper upbringing and she didn't cotton to Santos.

"It looks good for traveling," the tall man in the doorway said. The wind shifted Ruff Justice's long dark hair. Beard stubble now darkened his jaw. The eyes, icy blue, settled on Santos.

He knows, Amos thought. Oh, yes. He knows. Just like his brother. It was amazing that two such could have been whelped out of the same litter.

"I want those horses loaded up now. There's packs in the stable. Your brother must have made a lot of trips up here." Santos' dark eyes met Ruff's. "All for nothing, eh, Ruffin T. Justice?"

"Maybe." Ruff shrugged. "Maybe all for nothing." He started toward the stable, his movements catlike, lithe, sure. There was an added dimension to the man on this morning, a competence that was apparent in his every move. A special, electric aura.

"He knows," Santos said. "Watch him, Amos. Watch him very closely. If he does anything wrong, kill him. Don't wait if he starts to make trouble, because I think maybe this man can make plenty of trouble."

"What do you mean, kill him?" Sue Blackcastle said, stepping forward angrily. "What are you talking about? You won't touch those two men, not if I have anything to say about it."

"Well, you don't. Get ready to ride and keep your mouth shut," Santos said.

"Pop!"

"Sure, do what the captain says."

"Why the hell should I? I'm not some sailor on his ship."

"Please, Sue."

"Why, you're scared." She looked into Amos Blackcastle's eyes. "Why, damn me, you're scared, aren't you, Pop? Scared of this tattooed freak?"

"Yes," Amos said almost inaudibly. "I'm scared. Mind your pop, won't you?"

"Sure." Sue stepped back, her hand resting on her

father's chest. She glanced sharply at Santos. "I'll mind you, Pop. If I don't, maybe he'll kill both of us, too."

"Sue," Amos groaned.

"What's the matter, Pop? Can't stand the truth? Have you been lying so long that you can't take it anymore?"

"Damn you, girl," Santos said, stepping forward, lifting his hand.

"Don't do that!" Amos stepped back, and his rifle came up. His hands were shaking, but the gun was steady. "Don't hit the girl."

"Why, you pink fool." Santos laughed. "I do what I want. Give me that gun and—"

The rifle shot racketed down the slope. Santos looked in awe at Amos' rifle, but it wasn't Blackcastle who had fired. They looked downslope in time to see the Ute warriors rushing toward them, bursting out of the storm and the forest, their weapons stabbing tongues of flame.

"The cabin," Santos screamed.

Ruff Justice was in the stable, getting another pack for the horses. He heard the first shot, saw one of the pack animals run away in panic, Sandy Forrest clutching at, not finding the reins. Then he saw the Utes, their faces painted, their rifles spraying death.

"Get in here," he shouted at Sandy.

"The cabin."

"You won't make the cabin," Ruff Justice told him. "Get back in here and hope to God they don't see us."

It wasn't much of a hope. Half Moon's people were mad, and they had found something they needed badly—horses. There was also a place to shelter out of the brunt of the storm if they could just evict the whites.

They had every expectation of doing that. The rifles from the cabin were few, the guns from the pines many. Ruff Justice, armed with a length of

wood and his bowie knife, crouched in the near
darkness of the stable with a terrified Sandy Forrest.

Ruff nudged the kid and nodded toward a shovel
stuck in the corner of the stable. Sandy didn't think
much of that as a weapon, and it was true it wasn't
much against guns, but Ruff had seen some terrible
things done with the wide blade of a shovel.

The rifles continued to crackle and now, to top it
all, the snow began to fall again as the Utes assaulted
the cabin. They didn't want to burn it, not in this
weather; they wanted a lodge to lay up in while the
snows fell.

Ruff saw the Ute first. As he slipped in through
the stable's door, looking for horses and war trophies,
his rifle leveled, he blinked. The Ute blinked because
no matter how dark the day was outside, it was
darker within the stable, which was half cave. He
blinked, and it was the wrong thing to do.

Ruff Justice was on top of him, mauling him with
the razor-edged bowie, like a big cat striking, and the
steel of the blade found a major artery in the chest.
The Indian, his cry of agony muffled by the shriek
of the wind, toppled back, Ruff Justice falling with
him, clawing at the Winchester repeater in the Ute's
hand.

The second renegade was there before Ruff could
wrest the rifle from the dying Indian's hand. With a
scream as savage as any Indian's, Sandy Forrest, in
sheer terror, hurled himself at the Ute, slicing at his
belly with the shovel. Straight in went the sharpened
shovel blade, cutting a terrible eighteen-inch-wide
gash into the abdomen. The Ute threw back his head
and collapsed on the ground, and Sandy Forrest
beat at him with the shovel, battering his face and
chest until Ruff took him by the arm.

"He's dead, Sandy."

Ruff pulled the kid back, bent, and picked up the
second warrior's rifle, giving it to Sandy. This one

had also carried a buckskin sack filled with extra ammunition and they divided that up between them.

Now they were armed again, finally. Now they had a chance. A small one.

Ruff and Sandy went to the stable door. The Utes were flitting across the open spaces between the trees like dark ghosts, keeping up a constant barrage of rifle fire. Sandy lifted his rifle to his shoulder and sighted.

"Not yet," Ruff said, putting a hand on the barrel of the kid's gun. "Let's not let them know we're in here until we have to."

They waited silently, then, and watched. The Utes had regrouped in the trees again and were beginning to move toward the house, this time with more caution. They thought they knew the number of guns they were up against, not counting on there being fire from the stable.

The Utes were suddenly gone, every single one. Vanished into the snow. Ruff could feel electricity creep through his body, feel his gut tighten. He glanced at Sandy, nodding. Like an animal bunching its muscles to spring, the Utes had been waiting, and now with a cacophony of war cries, they rushed the house, their guns firing, the snow swirling and darting around them. Ruff opened fire.

He tagged his first man cleanly, from side to side through the chest; switched his sights and fired at the next target, missed, saw a bullet from the house get the Ute in the throat; switched to a third target and got the Indian as well.

Beside him Sandy was firing fast enough to melt the barrel of the Winchester he was using. Ruff put a calming hand on the kid's shoulder.

"Take it easy. There's time to aim."

Then Ruff got back to the aiming himself. They had the Utes in an unexpected and deadly cross fire, and the Indians were forced to pull back. Ruff dropped another of Half Moon's renegades who was too slow. Then they settled in to wait again.

"It gets my nerves," Sandy said anxiously. "What are they doing now? Are they coming back?"

"Just wait, watch. Don't think about it a lot. Keep your eyes moving."

"Sure. You've fought a lot of Indians, haven't you?"

"Too many." Far too many, Ruff thought at times. He had seen good men die for uncertain objectives, sometimes for the sake of simple blood lust. On either side.

The snow had halted again, and looking out across the clearing, they could see nothing but the bodies of the dead blanketed over with soft new snow.

"They're gone!"

"Uh-huh," Ruff answered, only half-believing it. It would have been more accurate to say they could no longer see any of the Utes. It wasn't the same thing.

They lay there stiff and cold for another half-hour, barely moving, Sandy twitching nervously at each whisper the wind made.

"Justice!" The cry was from the house. It was Santos, his voice hoarse and dry.

"What is it?"

"You got guns."

"That's right."

"Put them away. Throw them out here."

"You go to hell," Sandy Forrest shouted.

"You hear me, Justice?"

"We hear you," Ruff said. "It doesn't make any sense, though. Why would we?"

"We're going to move out while the Utes are holding back. Finish putting the packs on those horses and lead them to the house. We'll load the treasure now and be gone down the trail before they can get back."

"A pretty poor idea, Santos. We can hold out here for a long while."

"Without food? And what about you? How long

are you going to last over there when night falls with no fire, no blankets?"

Sandy looked worriedly at Ruff. Justice shook his head. "We'll stick it out. We've got a better chance than with the Utes."

"You're going to do what I say," Santos said loudly, his voice echoing to them.

"I don't think so. We've got the horses. We'll take our chances."

"I've got the girl," Santos crowed.

Ruff heard the shutter thrown open on the side window, and as he looked up, he saw Santos, his eyes wild, his fingers knotted into Sue Blackcastle's hair, his pistol shoved against her temple as she struggled to get free.

"I'll kill her, Justice. Kill her if you don't do what I say."

There wasn't a lot of choice. He was just mad enough to do it. Ruff and the kid ended up throwing their guns out into the yard. They followed, leading the horses with their empty packs.

Santos was in the doorway, gloating. Sue was leaning against the inside wall. Amos was sagged in the only chair in the cabin. "What's the matter with the old man?"

"Took a Ute bullet. He won't make it," Santos said offhandedly. "Get in here and start taking that gold out. Fast, before those damned Indians get back."

"This is never going to work, Santos."

"Shut up."

"How fast do you think those horses are going to move loaded down like this?"

"Do what I tell you." Santos was waving his gun around excitedly now, his eyes gleaming. "Girl, you help them."

She spun. "My father . . ."

"He's a goner. What're you going to do for him?"

"Why, damn you." Sue launched herself at Santos, but the pirate just slapped her away as if he were swatting an insect. She fell to the ground, her mouth trickling blood.

"Captain . . ." Amos was groaning, but Santos didn't pay any attention to him.

"Now get that gold loaded."

They started dragging it to the horses, their eyes going fearfully to the trees. The four horses were burdened with gold, with more gold, and still more. The snow began to fall and the wind increased, drifting the snow into the cabin, where they worked frantically, where an old man slowly bled to death.

In twenty minutes they were ready. Justice went to where Amos Blackcastle lay and he crouched down. "You all right, mate?" he asked.

"I'd take a cup of grog. Roland, don't let the captain get away with this."

"No," Ruff said, "I won't."

And then Amos Blackcastle died.

Sue sank to her knees and sat back, her hands on her lap, just staring in disbelief.

Santos growled at them. "Let's go. Let's go!"

They stepped outside and started leading the horses southward, through the thickening storm. Ruff led the way, followed by Sandy and Sue. Santos, leading Ruff's own gray, came last. The little mountain horse was loaded with hundreds of pounds of gold. The snow was deep, the altitude was killing, and they hadn't been fed or rested.

"These horses just aren't going to make it," Ruff shouted above the wind. Santos didn't even bother to answer. They trudged on and the snow fell.

They worked down through the gorge; the snow now covered the tangle of boulders and blown-down, weather-bleached trees, and they started up the long trail winding across the bald mountain.

Sue went down and Ruff helped her to her feet. Her eyebrows and lashes were rimed with frost, her face as white as flour, as the falling snow.

"He's crazy. I'm not going on."

"There's not much choice now, Sue," Ruff said grimly. "Look." She slowly turned her head, and then she could see them. Back a mile or so on their trail, twenty Indians pursuing them, running easily through the snow, rifles in their hands.

Santos had seen them as well. Now he cursed and swung the rifle to his shoulder, unleashing a barrage of gunfire. At that distance the bullets didn't even frighten the Indians. They kept on coming.

"Move it," Santos roared.

Justice got Sue to her feet and they trudged on. Every step was taken laboriously now. There was snow on the narrow trail, ice under that. They all recalled the horse that had misstepped and gone plummeting into that vast gorge.

They gasped for breath. The temperature continued to drop. Their lungs were alternately filled with fire and ice. Sue dropped to her knees in exhaustion twice more in the next mile.

They couldn't see the Utes now, but they knew they were back there, around a turn in the trail. Many scalps, horses, guns, a woman—everything needed to entice the warriors of Half Moon onward. They wouldn't be giving it up. Most Indians don't worry much about death. They believe you just go on pretty much as before in another world. Death in battle leads to a good life on that other plane. Why worry about achieving contentment and honor?

Justice didn't feel that confident. Some had predicted a slightly different fate for him.

The snow had shifted around and was driving into their faces. The wind was a mauling big beast, pressing them to the wall of the bluff, shrieking, howling, toying with them.

The white horse Santos had been riding went down hard on its side.

"Get it up, get it up," Santos screamed.

The horse lay thrashing about, unable to rise with

the ice, with the extreme load it carried. Its hooves
rang off stone and pawed at the air.

"It won't make it unless you get some of that gold
off."

"No!"

"Half at least."

"I said no."

"Then get it up yourself, dammit," Justice shouted
angrily. The wind drifted his long hair across his
face. Snow fell in a pale screen between his eyes and
Santos'.

"Half of it," the pirate said.

Ruff removed the heavy pack and helped the horse
to its feet; it stood quivering, cold, exhausted, and
confused. He began removing the gold and Santos
watched it fall, his black heart bleeding just a little.

They were losing time; the Utes were gaining
rapidly. Santos had to know that.

"If we kick it all over, we've maybe got a chance,"
Ruff said.

"Are you crazy? All of this for nothing?"

"Take a few pounds, a few good jewels."

"Go to hell. It's all mine. A few Indians aren't
going to take it from me. I've fought before. All of
them. Chinese bandits and Tripoli pirates, the British navy—"

"Maybe with cannon, at sea, but, Santos—"

"Get moving." He thrust the gun into Ruff's face.
"Get moving or you stay here. With the gold."

Ruff moved. His legs were leaden, his eyes hard
and cold, his ears and nose without feeling, his fingers clawlike.

"Insane," Sandy Forrest said. "He's mad. Ruff,
we're going to die. I want to tell you something."

"We're not going to die."

"Maybe not. I want to tell you anyway."

"I already know," Ruff said. "I think I already
know."

"But . . ." Ruff nodded and trudged on.

The trail was narrow here, too narrow. The horses with their human cargo had made it around the bend, but now, with the bulging packs hanging from their backs, with them having an uphill course instead of a downhill one ... they weren't going to make it, and that was that.

"What's going on? What's holding us up?" Santos demanded, fighting his way forward, past the halted horses.

"They can't get around the bend."

"Make them!"

"It's not physically possible. Would you look? We've got to unload."

"It's a trick. You want the gold. Like your brother. It's a trick!"

"Sure. I put the mountain there."

"Damn you to flaming hell," Santos shrieked, but he had gotten too close to Ruff. His thumb drew back the hammer of his Colt, but Ruff's hand was already coming up and he had Santos by the wrist, forcing that hand higher.

Sue screamed as the gun went off over Ruff's shoulder and the two men fell to the ground, locked in a deadly embrace. Below them the gorge yawned. Santos struck out in a mad fury, the pistol ringing off Ruff's skull. He got to his feet, the gun leveled, and Sue Blackcastle screamed again.

14

Justice's head was filled with pinwheels and the ringing of iron bells. He tried to get up but couldn't make it. It was a hazy moment before he knew who he was, where he was. Then the cold brought it back. The cold and the muzzle of the Colt revolver that Santos had shoved into his face.

Ruff's hand swept out and knocked the pirate's feet from under him. He toppled backward, his eyes wide, his hands clawing at the air.

And then he was gone, through the swirl of snow, a long scream issuing from deep within his throat. Gone. Ruff got shakily to his feet.

Sue Blackcastle was there, clinging to him. "Are you all right? Oh, God, I thought he'd split your skull."

Ruff held her for only a second. "Let's get moving," he said.

"But I thought—"

"Without the gold. It's your life or the treasure, Sue. Want to vote on it?"

"No."

"Sandy, send Santos' treasure after him."

Even Sandy Forrest was reluctant to do it. Justice had to urge him along. With his skinning knife Ruff cut the cinches and overboarded the packs. Gold and jewelry fell into the chasm at their feet, ringing and clattering away as the winter gods mocked with their shrill, howling laugher.

"Move it now," Ruff said.

"What about you?" Sue asked.

He had Santos' Winchester in his hands. "I'm going to give you a little time. Leave me my gray and then get out of here."

"All right." Sue kissed his cheek and then she mounted the pinto while Sandy Forrest stood staring at Ruff.

"Go on, Sandy. We haven't got another gun."

"I'll be at the ranch. I'll take Sue into town. We'll talk, get it straightened out."

"Get going," Ruff said angrily. Get it straightened out? There was no way talking was going to do that. Roland Justice had been murdered and the killer was still walking around unpunished. Santos was gone. Amos was gone. But the killer hadn't paid yet. Straighten it out? Yes, but not by talking about it.

The first Ute rounded the bend in the trail and Ruff Justice shot him through the chest. He settled in behind the sights, prone on the frozen trail. A second brave tried the same futile tactic and Ruff squeezed off a shot, pegging the Ute in the leg. He howled and fell back, dragging himself around the bend in the trail.

With any luck Ruff was going to be able to hold them off for quite a while. Long enough for Sandy and Sue Blackcastle to get away. With any luck.

It was cold, awful cold, with the snow falling and the wind raking him. His buckskins were frozen to the stone beneath him. The Utes were silent and Justice didn't know what they were up to. He looked overhead to see if there was any way they could flank him. Not likely. It was sheer and glassy up that slope, and above that was a shelf of snow nearly twenty feet deep. No one was going to move through that.

If only it wasn't so damned cold . . . He moved his legs, shifting to try to find some semblance of comfort. He held his hands in front of his mouth, blowing on them. It didn't do a lot of good. His breath seemed as cold as the falling snow. And the snow was falling heavily. Ruff could no longer see the bend in the trail. His visibility had been cut in half and then in half again. He doubted he could see more than fifteen feet. He glanced at the little gray horse which stood, ears pricked, snow-covered.

Make a try for it? Get out while the getting was good? It seemed like a good idea. The Ute suddenly bursting out of the snow delayed him. A bullet whined off the rock next to Ruff's face, spraying him with chips of ice and stone. Ruff triggered off . . . and the hammer fell on an empty chamber.

Justice rolled to one side, kicked out savagely, and dug at the Ute's stomach with his skinning knife. He touched vital organs and the Ute screamed out in agony, rolling slowly over the ledge, his rifle going with him. Ruff clutched at the weapon, but it was too late. It clattered away.

Now it was move or die. He was unarmed but for the knife, and the Utes weren't going to give up. He got to his feet and started toward the gray, aware of some distant rumbling in his ears, some shifting of the earth underfoot.

Then he realized what it was, and sheer, cold panic seized him.

Avalanche!

Ruff glanced up, and as he did, things started to come loose above him. He saw the wall of snow, vast and awesome, begin to slide forward. He leapt for the gray, but the horse shied away from him, turning and backing down the trail, one hind leg going over the edge of the precipice as Ruff fought to pull it forward with the reins.

There was no time. The little gray was crazed with fear. Ruff felt the earth move under his feet, heard the rumble like that of a distant locomotive, and he sprinted up the trail, leaving the gray to its terrible fate.

It came from above, snow and boulders and trees in a wall forty feet high, seeming much larger. Tons of moving earth, crushing everything in its way. The gray horse was gone, the trail was gone. Ruff Justice felt a head-sized stone strike his calf, and he cried out in pain. Snow tugged at his boots like receding surf, and he fought free, dragging his leg.

He staggered on, running up the icy trail for another hundred feet until he was sure he was out of the danger area. Then, panting, gasping, he sagged to the ground and stared in disbelief at the trail behind him.

A ramp of still-moving snow and ice, stone and debris had erased the trail, simply obliterated it. Snow dust rose in an eerie storm below, in the gorge where the treasure lay now buried by a thousand tons of snow and rock. The wind lifted the snow in great rooster tails and the new snow fell, gradually settling in.

The Utes were cut off. Maybe they had perished as well. Ruff couldn't be sure. But they were no longer a danger to him. Ruff got to his feet again, shivering, and his knee buckled on him. That rock had tagged him hard.

"How far, Justice? Twenty miles?" he asked himself.

Twenty miles or more back to any kind of shelter, and he had a bad leg. That, and the storm was coming in again.

"Stand here then and die," he told himself angrily. No, he wouldn't do that. He enjoyed living too much: the jokes, the good meals, the warm and lovely women waiting out there somewhere for him.

He turned and started on, fighting his way through the teeth of the storm toward a goal he had no right to expect to reach. It got worse as he walked on, and now the world was beginning to get dark. He just wasn't going to make it, that was all there was to it—he wasn't going to make it anywhere. He was going to be knocked down by the wind and covered by the snow.

And Roland's killer would still be alive.

There was an irony there, especially since Ruff now knew who it was. He knew, and he couldn't do a thing about it. Through the snow he saw something dark smudged against the prevailing whiteness of the land, and he staggered that way, moving now through knee-deep snow. He had no idea what it was, but anything might offer some shelter. Just a little—something to break the wind, to offer some hope of survival.

It was a small stand of pines and Ruff couldn't recall any on their backtrail. With stark fear he realized that he must have somehow gotten off the mountain trail and was now wandering lost.

"All right." He looked to the skies. "Sit it out, Justice. Sit the night out. Maybe it'll clear by morning." Maybe it wouldn't. Maybe it wouldn't matter at all to Ruff Justice if it did. The temperature was going to drop to thirty or forty below as the sun sank, and there was no living in that sort of weather, not out in the open without a fire.

He shook his head. A fire? Could he start one in this wind? His brain seemed not to be functioning properly, either because of the extreme cold or because of the rap on the head Santos had given him.

He looked around. He was in the dark pines and the sky above was getting darker. Trees meant wood. All frozen and damp . . . matches? Yes, he hadn't gone without matches for years, tightly wrapped in a small oilskin packet.

Ruff moved on deeper into the forest, his teeth chattering, trying to get out of the wind. He didn't have much luck at it. Finally he did stop; he had to. It was dark and cold and there was nowhere to go. He crawled into a clump of pine-sheltered boulders and sagged there. Digging beneath the snow, he found a thick bed of pine needles. They were damp, soaked through, but a little deeper was another layer, somewhat drier—and beneath an outcropping in the rocks, another layer, very nearly dry.

The snow filtered down through the trees. Thunder shook the forest. The earth trembled. Lightning spat across the skies. Ruff fumbled for the extra cartridges he had stuffed into his pockets, withdrew a handful and bit the bullets from them, pouring the black powder onto the pile of carefully constructed pine needles and small twigs. His hands were so cold they were virtually useless. He tried to strike a match and had it break in his hand. Again he tried, scraping the head of the match across a small stone. The match flared up, and turning his eyes away, he dropped it onto the gunpowder.

It went up with a brilliant flash and Ruff began puffing at it, trying to nurture the small flames, trying to urge the thing, the life-giving, yellow-red tongues to grow.

He prodded it with tiny twigs, with the inner, fibrous bark torn from the pine trees near at hand, and slowly, so slowly, the fire grew, blazing against the night, and as it grew, Ruff fed it. A little, and then, as it became more voracious, all it would stand as the fire blazed up and roared and crackled and spit and steamed against the night sky.

And he sat by it, hunched, staring, unsleeping. He would not sleep, for then the fire might die; and if it did, then Ruff Justice would also perish.

The snow fell and the fire glowed, twisting and writhing against the overpowering strength of the night, and Ruff Justice stared at the flames, seeing the face of his brother's killer and that of the dark-haired woman, and at times they merged and became the same.

Dawn came and it was pink and orange, pale blue.

Dawn came and the man with the snow on his shoulders and lap, with his hair all frosted and tangled, the man who sat before the cold pile of blackened wood looked skyward, squinting into the brilliant, dancing light that beamed through the dark pines.

The storm was gone and he was living. Living still, a stalking thing, a blood-hungry, angry thing seeking vengeance. Ruff sat a long while, hours perhaps, looking at the sun, at the dead fire. Then he rose, staggering against the rocks as he fought for balance, his legs numb and sore, his head spinning.

He stood there, and then, with the greatest of efforts, he forced himself onward. The killer was still waiting and he was Retribution.

He came out of the trees and stood facing the endless miles of snow field, the towering rocky peaks. He looked again to the sun, got his bearings, and started on, trudging southward, thinking of nothing but his goal as he left deep tracks across the long fields of virgin snow.

Looking upslope and along a twisting ridge where a few wind-flagged cedars survived the harshness of the Colorado winters, Ruff saw the bald mountain. It looked to him like the back of Ute's Thumb, and if it was, he could save many hours by cutting up and over the ridge. The snow would be deeper there, the going harder, yet he figured it was worth a try.

He climbed higher yet, walking along the steep side of the sawtooth. Above him the wind lifted horses' tails of snow from the pinnacle. Here and there a cedar grew, tiny, gnarled, but nothing else.

Ruff's leg ached, his head hurt. He had to pause frequently for breath as the altitude was starting to get to him. He plodded on, fighting through snow to his knees and sometimes to his waist in the hollows.

It was an agonizing, bitterly cold trek, one of the most difficult days Ruff could remember. He had only his thoughts of vengeance to keep him warm, to keep him plodding onward.

At noon he crested the ridge, looked out across the tangle of mountains and canyons, hogbacks, and forested hills to see nothing identifiable, except one far-distant something that might have been a wisp of smoke. He started on down, heading for easier ground.

Once he reached the timber, the going was better. He stayed in the trees where the snow was thinner, the wind cut. Ruff looked to the skies frequently, fearing fresh snowfall, but it seemed to be holding off. He also feared the darkness. He didn't want to spend another night out here. Not one like the last night.

He wasn't going to have to, he decided suddenly.

"Damn me, look at that."

He was standing on the edge of the forest looking at a little, tight-looking, windowless shack. Above, the sundown was beginning to color the skies. It had been a long and wearying day.

He started plodding across the snowfield, noticing that the snow around the shack was packed down, indicating use, recent use. No one was there now, however, and as Ruff went inside, he silently thanked whoever had built this place in such an isolated, lonely location.

There was food in the pantry. Flour, sugar, coffee, and tins of beef and fruit. Justice wanted a fire, wanted one badly for the hot food and the warmth but caution urged him to eat from the tins, to leave the cabin dark.

He wolfed down the beef and a tin of plums and tossed the cans in a huge wooden box full of empty cans in the corner. The rattle hadn't died away before he heard the horses outside.

Ruff looked around urgently. He had no gun and he wasn't in shape to compete with whoever was riding up. He had no reason to believe it was necessarily enemies. But then again he had few friends in these mountains.

He saw no place to hide, so he simply stepped behind the door. If they saw his footprints outside, they would know he was there, but it was getting dark and there was a chance they wouldn't.

He heard voices booming and the door swung open.

". . . son of a bitch watch his own animal from now on. I damn near froze to death last night."

Ruff stepped out from behind the door, hooked his forearm around the man's throat, kicked the door shut, and held the deadly little skinning knife to the throat of John Dirk.

"Shuck the gun or die. Your choice."

"Justice!"

"Now." Now, before the man outside could join them.

Dirk felt the point of the knife bite in a little deeper and he reached inside his heavy coat to unbuckle his gunbelt. It dropped to the floor, and Ruff shoved him away.

Dirk staggered across the room and Justice snatched up the worn Remington pistol he had been carrying.

"Say, Dirk . . ." The gunman stepped into the cabin to find himself face to face with Ruff Justice. His eyes lowered to the gun Ruff held and his hands slowly went up, a thin smile on his lips.

"You got me. Take it."

"Unbuckle it for me, would you?" Ruff asked quietly. He heard Dirk move, saw the foreman reach for something under the bunk, and Ruff fired, his bullet plowing up splinters from the wooden floor. Dirk pulled back with a yipe, holding a hand that looked like a porcupine.

"Damn you. My hand's ruined."

"Not yet. I shoot even closer. Don't try that again."

The gunman chuckled. His well-oiled twin Colts dropped to the floor. "You two take off your coats as well," Ruff said. Eyeing Dirk, he backed to the bunk. His toe searched for and found the scattergun the foreman had been reaching for.

Dirk was stripped of his coat now and he sat at the crude table the cabin was furnished with, pulling the splinters from his hand with his teeth.

"You do know me?" the gunman in black asked Ruff Justice.

"I've seen you."

"My name is Bo Henry. I wanted you to know that, Justice."

"Why?"

"I think a man should know who kills him."

"Is that what you're going to do, Bo Henry?"

"Yes." The man in black was very serious. His little eyes shined. "That's what I'm going to do. And you can tell all my friends in hell that Bo Henry done it."

"Maybe you'll be telling them yourself, Bo. Sit down. You're making me nervous."

Bo sat there staring at Ruff, who barred the cabin door, kicked the two men's coats aside, and crouched near the fireplace, figuring he may as well be warm now. He wasn't going to keep his presence a secret.

"Where you been, Ruff Justice? You look a little beat up?"

Ruff didn't answer Henry's question. He felt a little beat up, though. Beat up, exhausted, sleepy— God, he was sleepy. Maybe the fire had been a mistake. It was too warm and his eyelids felt suddenly heavy.

That wouldn't do. He moved away from the fire, pistol still in hand. "Bo, I want you to tie Dirk up for me."

"Do what?" Dirk said, his big head coming up. He still had his bloody hand cradled.

"Take his belt, his scarf, tear the sleeves off his

shirt if you have to. Tie him wrists and ankles, hands behind the chair. Make a nice figure-eight knot there, good and tight."

"Afraid of falling asleep, Justice?"

"Do it, Bo Henry."

"Sure." Henry shrugged. He got to work on a protesting John Dirk.

"Where's the Morgan, Dirk?" Ruff asked softly. He was perched on the corner of the table, watching Bo Henry work.

"I don't know what the hell you mean."

Ruff backhanded him and Dirk's head snapped around. He tried to get up out of his chair, but he was already tied fairly well and Ruff just pushed him back.

"I want to know where the Morgan horse is. Bo Henry?"

"I don't know," the gunman said.

"Dirk, you were talking when you came in about someone watching his own animal. I figure you had to mean King Forrest and that Morgan horse."

"Figure what you want," Dirk growled.

"I'm tired, Dirk. Tired and beat up. I spent last night outside. It was snowing, Dirk. It was cold as sin. I didn't like it much. Tonight I'm spending inside. But maybe you aren't."

"What do you . . . ?"

"Maybe both of you are going to camp out. Would you like that, John Dirk? Bo Henry?"

"You wouldn't do that, Justice. I know you, you're a *gentleman*," Dirk said.

"Yes? Well, I am, up to a point. I'm a gentleman when I'm dealing with people who have the decency to act like gentlemen and ladies. But when I'm with folks like you, Dirk, I can get awfully tired, awfully ungentlemanly. No, you'll tell me, Dirk. You'll tell me now or I'll put you out there for the night. And it's going to be a cold one. Real cold."

"Damn you, Ruff Justice. Damn you to hell. I'd like to—"

"Are you going to tell me?"

"Yes, damn you. I'll tell you where it is."

And he did.

15

After Bo Henry had tied Dirk up, Ruff tied the gunman similarly. They weren't real comfortable in those wooden chairs, but they were a lot more comfortable in there with the fire than they would have been outside in the bitterly cold night.

Ruff himself moved the bunk nearer to the fire and lay down, his head propped up on a bedroll belonging to one of the Forrest men; and with a light blanket up under his chin, his pistol in his hand, he spent the night in supreme comfort.

Dirk and Bo Henry were all complaints in the morning. Ruff ate first and then untied the two so that they could eat as he stood watching them, gun in hand.

"Eat plenty. We've got some work to do this morning."

"Like what?" Dirk growled.

"We're going to be cowboys, Dirk. You recall that kind of work, don't you? You might have done it once or twice before you became bully boss. How about Bo Henry, though? He doesn't look much like a cowboy."

"What do you have in mind?" Bo Henry asked. "The horses?"

"That's right. You boys are going to help me take

them in. The Morgan and the other horses that belonged to my brother."

"You'll never keep them."

"We'll see about that."

"If you think I'm going to help you—" Bo Henry began.

"Those that don't want to work can stay behind."

Henry looked at him nervously. "What do you mean?"

"I'll just tie you up safe and sound and leave you here."

"No one would find me. Not up here."

"No.' Ruff shook his head. "I wouldn't think so."

They rode out half an hour later, Ruff on a spare pack animal.

They found the horses in a small sheltered valley ringed by boulders and lodgepole pines. The day was cold, but the valley, sheltered as it was, was comparatively mild. There was hay strewn about the snow. Someone had been taking care of a valuable article.

And there it was, big and dark, long-haired with the winter, muscles in chest and haunches quivering, showing the lines that Justin Morgan had bred for. The stallion was larger than other Morgans Ruff had seen, almost a freak, but, Lord, there was dynamite waiting to explode in those muscular legs!

It stood, steam drifting from its nostrils, ears pricked, watching the approach of the men. Around him was his harem, all watching warily.

"There any trouble herding them?" Ruff wanted to know.

"No. Not if he knows he's goin' home," Dirk said grudgingly. "He goes and the others follow. Only problem we had was keeping them off RJ range."

"All right." Dirk was still unhappy, but he and Ruff had had a nice polite chat on the way out. Justice had explained that in this territory men had been known to be hanged for taking a horse, and that maybe, if Dirk would agree to a little cooperation, Justice would consider this more of a loan where Dirk was concerned. Dirk had thought it over and then agreed reluctantly, saying he wasn't suited to large neckties.

Bo Henry wasn't making any deals with anyone. He wanted to kill Ruff Justice. Period. It was his way of dealing with life's little problems. Consequently Dirk's hands were free to help Ruff move the horse herd out of the valley, but Bo Henry on a long lead rope, sat with his hands strapped together behind his back.

"I guess you got the whole thing figured out by now," John Dirk said as they rode along, pushing the herd, which, true to Dirk's prediction, was heading almost unguided home to the RJ ranch.

"I think so. You were there?"

"I was there when they killed your brother, yes. But I didn't know it was going to happen. Crazy. That's what it was. There was no reason for it."

"The horse didn't enter into it?"

"Ah, hell, no. I think King Forrest took it away so's not to leave a reminder, but that wasn't the cause of it in no way."

No, Ruff had figured it wasn't. They rode slowly down the long slopes. The skies were mostly clear, the sun glittering on the new snow, long clouds interrupting the brilliant display intermittently. The air was clean and cold, rich with pine scent. The Morgan stallion bounded through the belly-deep snow, taking it easily, making a game of its homecoming, the rest of the herd following in its tracks.

Ruff glanced back at Bo Henry, who was scowling deeply, his hat tugged low.

"What's his main function?" Ruff asked.

"Killing people."

"What's King Forrest got him around for?"

Dirk kind of shrugged. "Maybe he thought some-

one like you would be coming down the trail after
your brother got killed, huh?"

"I guess that's it." Yes, after the murder King
Forrest had known someone would be coming, sooner
or later. He knew that the men at Stokes' store had
written the army. There was a brother out there
somewhere—Ruff Justice—and he would be coming.

They rode on, watching the poetry the horses
sketched against the snow, paying little attention to
Bo Henry. They should have paid a little more.

The outlaw was simmering, his anger decaying all
caution. He despised Justice, hated John Dirk for
"turning traitor." If he got the chance . . . And he
was within inches of having that chance. The ropes
chafed at his wrists as he stretched the knots and
stretched them again. Dirk had tied them, and Dirk
had, of course, done a rather sloppy job. It looked
good. When Justice had tested the bonds, Bo Henry
had flexed his muscles to pull against them, making
the knots seem much tighter than they were.

Now he was working at them, his fingers cramping
as he strained to reach the knots, struggled to untie
them. Then he felt the end of one knot slip free.
Carefully he tugged at it, trying to remain naturally
upright in the saddle. He saw Dirk laugh at something Justice said, and he cursed silently.

What the hell kind of man abandons the brand?
What the hell kind of man takes up with the other
side? The bastard deserved to die, and he would—
after Ruff Justice.

The knot slipped free and Bo Henry felt the rope
uncoil just a little. He jerked at the bonds until the
rope fell nearly free. Only then did he glance back
toward his saddlebags. Slowly he reached back, found
the buckle, and opened the right-hand bag; his
anxious, searching hands dipped inside, finding the
cool walnut butt of the spare Colt revolver.

Bo Henry sat up again, a smile playing on his lips,
the gun in his right hand. And he thought, Time's

almost come, Mister Justice. It's nearly time to say hello to the boys in hell for Bo Henry.

It was another hour to the ranch. The cabin was as Justice had left it. There was more snow on the ground. The door to the cabin was open as they rode up, letting the horses run free across the meadow, content to be home once more.

"Company?" Dirk asked, nodding toward the open door.

"I don't know."

Justice swung down and walked cautiously toward the house. There was no one inside, nothing. There was a note on the table written in a childish scrawl.

Dear Mr. Justice,

Sandy brought me over and we found the dog. He was all right, but not real good. As he was still weak and hungry, I took him with me. I don't know if you'll read this note or not as the last time I saw you you might have been dead. If you ain't, thank you for killing Santos. If ever a man needed it, he did. Your friend,

Sue Blackcastle

The shot brought Ruff's head around. He rushed to the door of the cabin in time to see John Dirk topple heavily from the saddle, his face a mask of blood. Smoke still rose from the pistol in Bo Henry's hand and Ruff threw himself to one side as that pistol spoke again.

A .44 bullet thudded into the door frame and a second passed through the house to shatter the window. Ruff, on his belly, rolled to one side, fired out the door, and rolled back as Bo Henry put another round through the barrel of his Colt, one that burned a long groove in the floorboards inches from Ruff's arm.

He was good. Bo Henry was a snake, but he was

Bo Henry staggered back three steps and then he stepped into the doorway to hell.

Ruff Justice holstered the gun and walked forward across the snowy yard. When he reached the open grave, he stood looking down at the twisted figure of Bo Henry. Then, shaking his head, he turned away and started for his horse.

It was time to be done with this, time to finish what had to be done in these mountains. He swung up onto the horse and turned it toward the Forrest ranch.

16

·····➤━━◆━━◄·····

The ranch rested in the tiny valley, pretty and prosperous-appearing, neat and filled with gradual rot. Ruff Justice sat just looking at the house for a long while before he started down the slope toward the Forrest ranch.

The little stream was fringed with ice as Ruff's horse clattered across the narrow bridge and up into the yard of the house. In the back a few cowboys in sheepskin coats stood around a breaking corral, watching the wrangler. There wasn't much work to be done just now. Ruff saw heads turn as he swung down and walked slowly toward the porch, feeling the weight of his vengeance on his shoulders.

The first one out the door was Sue Blackcastle. She had on a light-blue dress, her blond hair coiled up on top of her head, and she stood, hands on hips, watching the man in buckskins.

"Damn me," she said. "Mister Ruffin Justice, you made it out of there."

"Yes, I did."

Sue came to the top step and threw her arms around Ruff, hugging him. She stepped back. "I feel it. Something's wrong."

"That's right," Ruff said.

"It's not over yet."

"No, Sue, it's not over."

"Get off my property. I told you not to come back."

Ruff lifted his eyes slowly, knowing he would find the bull there, the big, stove-up old man, King Forrest. There was a shotgun in Forrest's hands.

"No good, Forrest," Ruff said. "You can't solve your problem with a gun."

"I'll solve you, all right."

"Maybe, but it won't end things, will it? It won't finish the troubles."

"Dad . . ." Sandy Forrest was there now, and behind him, hidden in the shadows, Natalie stood dark and beautiful and mysterious. Sandy Forrest was standing next to his father. His eyes were like a dog's, hurt yet faithful. The kid had aged some since Ruff had first seen him. There were bruises on his face, a few raw new scars on his hands. He had been out with the big boys, fought a little hard weather, a few Indians. "Father, it's no good. I think I know Ruff Justice a little now. He isn't here to destroy things."

"How can anything be done if someone isn't destroyed?" the old man asked miserably. The muzzle of his shotgun slowly lowered. He shook his head sadly, heavily. "You know all about it?" he asked Ruff.

"I think so."

"Come on in, then. Come into my house."

King Forrest turned and went heavily in, Sandy helping him. Natalie stepped aside and watched, her eyes unreadable.

"What the hell is this?" Sue Blackcastle wanted to know. "What's happening?"

"You'll see."

"I'll see, hell. Tell me."

"Come on." He took her arm and turned her toward the door. There was the sudden scrabbling of heavy feet on the wooden steps, and as Ruff turned, the big dog leapt up, licking at his face, wriggling with joy, running down the steps to dart around in circles with sheer exuberance.

"He's all right," Sue said. She still held Ruff's arm, looking up at him. "How about you, tall man?"

"I'll make it." The dog had come back and it lay on the sunny porch as Ruff stroked its head briefly, seeing the bullet groove where Santos had shot it. Santos, who wouldn't be shooting anyone or anything anymore.

Natalie was still watching. Ruff looked at her, nodded, and went on in, Sue beside him. The two women exchanged a dueling glance.

In the study—as King Forrest called his drinking room—the two men waited, one old, one young. There were leather chairs scattered around, longhorns mounted on the wall, a few heavy books on a shelf, an Indian blanket, and King Forrest behind the desk with a bottle of bourbon in one hand, a glass in the other. The scattergun sat on his desk.

"Sit down," Forrest said, waving at a chair. He looked very old suddenly. "One of my men just rode in from the RJ. He says John Dirk and Bo Henry are dead."

"That's right."

"You kill them?"

"Henry killed Dirk. I killed Henry."

"Didn't think anyone could beat Henry in a fair fight." King Forrest drank his whiskey down at a gulp.

"Anybody can be beat at any game," Ruff answered. "You've lived long enough to know that."

"Yes." King poured another glass of whiskey and sat staring at the amber liquid. "You're right."

Ruff took a seat across from Forrest. Behind him was a large, high window; from there Forrest could oversee his small empire, now deep in snow. Sandy was in a chair in the corner, legs crossed, staring down at his hands. Natalie had come up behind

Ruff. She rested a hand briefly on his shoulder and then moved away; Ruff watched her go, wondering.

"We're all here," King said.

"All of us?" Ruff asked.

"All that matter."

"All right," Ruff said with a shrug. "My brother was killed, King Forrest. He was killed in these mountains, and you know who did it. He was killed and just shoved into the ground. You took away his property, but we'll let that slide for now. I've got it back anyway."

"Yes, I thought you'd get it back. Fine-looking stallion, isn't it?"

"It is. Maybe we can do some dickering after this is done—if you want to buy the herd."

"We'll talk."

"Sure. For now let's talk about Roland. He was in love with your daughter." Ruff looked at Natalie, so beautiful and devoted. She turned her eyes away.

"I loved him, too," Natalie said to no one.

"I know that," Ruff said quietly. "I'm sorry." He returned his attention to King Forrest. "Someone saw the murder, an old Indian named Packrat. Of course, he's dead now. But he did manage to spread it around that a woman had killed Roland."

Sandy hung his head. Natalie stared at nothing. King Forrest poured another glass of liquor. Only Sue seemed not to know where the conversation was leading. She turned from the window, holding the drapery loosely.

"You, King Forrest, you could have prevented this mess," Ruff said.

"I thought I was doing right," he answered. "Things just got worse, year by year."

"Was it her?" Sue asked suddenly. She pointed at the dark-haired woman in the corner. "She killed Roland Justice?"

"Yes," Ruff said. "She did it. She loved a man who

didn't love her. That's a deadly situation. She killed
Roland. Didn't she, Sandy? King?"

The dark-haired woman shrilled a cry. She leapt
across the room, her hair tumbling free, her eyes
going wide, her lip curled back to flash white teeth,
sharp and bright. She reached for the scattergun on
her father's desk. She started to bring it up and
around toward Ruff Justice.

The gun in Sue Blackcastle's hand spoke twice and
the shotgun clattered free. The dark-haired woman
folded up and fell to the floor, dead. Sue screamed
and threw the gun away.

"I didn't mean to. God, she was going to kill you,
Ruff. I'm sorry." And then Sue was in Ruff's arms
and he stroked her head. Sue had seen a lot of death
lately, too much, and she wasn't quite as tough as she
wanted people to think.

King Forrest had gotten out of his chair, his face
contorted first with shock, then agony. He fell as he
tried to rise and now he crawled to his daughter. He
cradled her head on his lap. Blood ran from her
mouth. He petted her and cooed to her. Ruff had to
turn away.

"Darlin', darlin'. Where's Natalie, honey? Where is
she?" King Forrest asked. Sue turned, her expression befuddled.

"Am I crazy or are they?" she asked.

"Not they. She. She was crazy. I knew when she
slashed at me with a knife . . . but that's not Natalie
Forrest, is it, Sandy?"

The kid shook his head. He was frozen in his chair
like a carved wooden figure. King was still petting
his daughter's head, only her eyes were staring up at
him unseeing, uncaring.

"Who in God's name is it?" Sue asked. A bunch of
cowboys had appeared in the doorway now, answering the sounds of the shots. King sat with the girl on
his lap, staring at nothing. It was up to Sandy to tell
them what to do.

"It's all right. Find my sister, will you?"

"There's no need," the voice from behind the men said. Natalie came forward then, and on her wrists were broken ropes. Her face was bruised. "Dead?"

"Yes."

"Poor Nanette."

"Twins?" Sue Blackcastle asked.

"Yes, twins. Only something was wrong with this one, with Nanette. She wasn't right in the head. When Roland came into these mountains, he and Natalie fell in love. Nanette felt cheated." Ruff looked to Natalie, who nodded. "She started sneaking around—I don't know what she would have done, you figure it out. I don't think Roland knew there were two of them."

"No," Sandy Forrest said. "We always kept Nanette away from people. No one outside the family was to know we had madness in the house."

"She was jealous of her sister, to put it plainly. And in time it became obsessive. She killed Roland. He walked right into her gun, probably. He would have thought she was Natalie. He thought Natalie . . . was wrong."

"I couldn't tell him," Natalie said, breaking into tears. "They wouldn't let me. They said it had to be our secret, and besides, Roland wouldn't marry me if he knew that there was madness in our family. As a result," she said, eyes downcast, "he died."

"After that they had to cover it up. They tried," Ruff said.

"But you knew," Sue said.

"I guessed, mostly. At first it was just a feeling. When Natalie tried to stab me—the woman I thought was Natalie—it all came clear. She kept calling me Roland, although Natalie knew I was Ruff Justice. And there was the other thing, of course—"

"What other thing?" Sue asked.

"Why, Natalie is right-handed. Nanette is left-handed." He looked at Natalie. "Isn't that right?"

"Yes, but . . . how did you know?"

Ruff didn't answer. Later when he and Sue Blackcastle were riding back to the RJ together she asked him the same question.

"That was when you first suspected? But how did you know?"

"Easy. I'd seen Natalie doing things around here. Placing the flowers and such. I knew she was right-handed."

"But Nanette? You never ever saw her before today."

"Oh, yes, I did," Ruff answered. "One night she came. She came and she stayed with me. Believe me," Ruff said with a wink, "you can tell a right-handed woman from a left-handed one in bed, and the one I spent the night with was not Natalie Forrest."

17

"Well?"

"Woman, you confound my theory," Ruff Justice said. "Ambidextrous."

"That's right," Sue said, snuggling closer in the bed. "And you like it."

"I like it, but it's a good thing I didn't meet you before I met Nanette. It would have ruined everything."

"I think you made it all up just to tease me anyway," she said, kissing Ruff's chest, one of her talented hands finding its way to his groin, where it began enthusiastically reviving his interest.

"You're right," Ruff said, kissing her shoulder and then her throat. "I made it up."

"Oh, now you are lying," Sue said. She threw her leg up over him and inserted him easily between her thighs. She gave a little sigh. "You're beautiful, Ruffin."

"Yes? You say that because I shower you with gifts," he answered, drawing her down on top of him, his hands resting on her buttocks, feeling the clench and sway of the muscles there. She was beautiful, was Sue Blackcastle. A diamond in the ruff. Or vice versa.

She had made a promise a while back, a promise

to show her truly remarkable breasts to him, and she had lived up to her word. Entering the cabin, she had turned, slowly unbuttoning her shirt. Ruff had closed the door, watching, waiting, feeling the slow thickening and lengthening of his shaft.

"There. All right?"

They bobbed free, strawberry-tipped, jutting, milky breasts, and Ruff went to her. Her head lolled back on her neck as he kissed her breasts and her hands dropped between his legs.

"Only a man, as I said," Sue cracked.

"Isn't that enough?"

"Yes." She laughed, but there was too much emotion in her to sustain the laugh, and Ruff carried her to the bed. Then she showed him the other gadgets and nooks she carried around with her, a softly molded cleft which Ruff kissed gently, tenderly; the blond, downy patch between her thighs where a tiny bud, pink and stiffening, lay awaiting the attention of his lips.

"Gifts . . ." She lay on her side now, her eyes glazed, her body rocking against his, her fingers groping for Ruff, finding him.

"The ranch."

"Oh, the ranch. I thought you meant—"

"That's not a gift. Have to take it with me," Ruff Justice said. "Only a loan."

"You wouldn't consider making it more than that?"

"I've considered; I can't."

"All right. Let's use the damn thing while we can. Poke it up there, Ruffin. Again. God, that's good! Oh, Jesus." She shuddered a little, and Ruff held her while her body trembled away its fulfillment.

"You'll be lonely here," he said at length.

"Maybe. At least I'll have a home. With those Morgans, I guess I'll have more than I ever had—a little deeper, honey—and I feel bad about it in a way. It's your herd."

"It was Roland's, not mine. I don't think I'd want

to see that stallion day after day," he said. "And I don't have the time to raise horses properly, to show them, curry them, to breed them."

"It's a shame, too," Sue said.

"Yes?"

"Yes. You're such a good breeder."

Ruff tried to be. He rolled her onto her back, and as Sue's legs lifted straight into the air, he gave her the length of his breeding, driving it in to the hilt as she lay there, her hands making tiny clutching movements, her head rolling from side to side, her eyes half-closed, her lips moving in meaningless ways, until Ruff felt his own completion battering at the door of need and he let it free again. Then, he again lay against Sue Blackcastle, and her legs lifted and wrapped around him, holding him there.

Later they got up, and without bothering to dress, they ate before the roaring fire. The dog watched them from the corner of the room.

"He'll be company for you," Ruff commented.

"Not enough."

"No, I understand that, but he'll at least have people. Poor dog's been through a lot."

"I thought you didn't care about him," Sue said.

"Did you?"

"Sure. Why, you were always trying to give him away. You wouldn't even give him a name."

"Well, what's a dog need a name for?"

Sue watched Ruff curiously for a minute. He thought how lovely she looked naked, across the table at mealtime.

"You're a faker, Ruff Justice."

"Of course."

"I mean it. You care about the dog, about Natalie, about old King Forrest, even about me, for all I know."

"Now your imagination is getting the best of you," Ruff joked.

"Sure," Sue said. "There's no reason for you to have given me this ranch."

"I told you, I can't handle it. I've got to get back to Lincoln."

"Well, why do you? What kind of life is that? A man with any brains would see that this could be a far better life. Beautiful country, good stock, willing, ambidextrous female."

"You're right, I've got no brains.

"No, I guess not." Sue was thoughtful, watching the tall man. You can't force a man like that to do anything, but damn him, why would he want to leave? "You could at least take the stallion. Sell him. That's a lot of money, Justice."

"Who would I leave it to? Sue, I'll tell you straight out. I knew the madness in Nanette Forrest because I'm a little mad myself. I was put on earth to live, and I want to live. Danger is a part of that to me. Women, good food, sleeping in a sunny meadow, a fast horse—yes, all of that is important, but I have to have that excitement. I have to know I'm on the ragged edge of survival to feel that I'm truly alive. Yes," he said quite seriously, "and one day they'll take me and bury me and talk about me. But until then I have to do it my way. The thing is—money, permanence aren't much to me."

"You're suicidal."

"Probably." Ruff shrugged.

"And," Sue Blackcastle said with surprising perceptiveness, "there is somewhere a woman who is the real thing to you."

"Maybe," Ruff answered.

"Oh, hell, Justice. It don't matter. Likely I'll just go ahead and trap that Sandy Forrest into marrying me. Now there's a gullible young man, and a fairly wealthy one."

"He's a good kid, Sue."

She sighed. "Yes, he's that. Poor bastard. If he knew . . ."

"And you're a good woman. Don't tear yourself down."

Her blue eyes lifted to his, and they were damp and bittersweet. "You think I'm all right? Think I'd make a man a good wife?"

"I know you would, Sue."

"Yes? Then come on over here. I need a little more practice."

Ruff did so. He went to her and bent to kiss her shoulder.

The door popped open and Santos stood there, gun in hand. Sue screamed and pulled away. Ruff Justice, naked, weaponless, stood facing the apparition.

"Not dead." Santos laughed, his voice weird, crazy. There were weather blisters on his lips, his cheeks, great savage scabs. His hair had fallen out on one side. He was dressed in rags. His tattooed torso showed through the tears in his shirt—yellow eyes and dragons' tongues, sailing ships and tigers with fangs bared.

"I'm not dead," he said. "Fell a long way. The gold—it was there and I went for it, and then it was gone. The snow from above. Avalanche," Santos said, closing the door behind him, shutting out the stars beaming over the mountains. "Avalanche came and washed the gold away. A prince's ransom. It was all mine, but you and your brother took it from me. I had the world in my hand and you took it and stepped on it."

"Santos, it wasn't like that," Ruff said quietly.

"Everything I wanted. Had it all in the palm of my hand. Justice, you took it." His eyes were quite mad. He had frostbite marks on his arms, face, and chest. He was going to lose an ear, a nose, his fingers, if he lived.

"Kill you," Santos said, and the tattooed man lifted his pistol with both hands.

The dog was a gray flash from the corner of the cabin where it had crouched, waiting. It knew. It knew this one was the one who had shot him, knew this human was the one who would kill his master.

The growl was deep and terrible, the leap too quick to follow, the savage attack incredibly bloody as the dog tore the throat out of Santos and the pirate fell dead to the floor, the dog hunched and snarling, watching.

"Easy," Ruff said. He put a hand on the dog's back. "It's over."

And it was. There was nothing left to do but remove what was left of the madman, and wrap the warm, loving woman in his arms and pass the long cold winter night.

WESTWARD HO!

**The following is the opening section from the
next novel in the gun-blazing, action-packed new
Ruff Justice series from Signet:**

RUFF JUSTICE #17: DRUM ROLL

1

The sergeant wore a black armband, and when he
spoke to the jailer his voice was very soft. Beyond the
gray stone wall of the cell a muffled drum roll was
being played. It was muted and dry, like the death
rattle in a man's throat.

"Bixby."

Sergeant Albertson unlocked the iron door and
Bixby just glared at him. The ponderous man in the
first sergeant's uniform stepped past Albertson, the
jailer.

"Time to go," Sergeant Mack Pierce said. Bixby,
in prison stripes, spat on the floor and deliberately
looked away. Outside, the drum sounded again.

"You go to hell," Bixby said.

"I guess maybe one of us is. Get up, Bix. Don't
make us carry you out. Be a man for a change."

That stung Bixby, and he rose to his feet as if he
would take a swing at the first sergeant, but Fort
Lincoln's first shirt, despite his bulk and apparent
obesity, was a lot of man. Three hundred pounds of
man, and if it wasn't all muscle, it was all determina-
tion, everyone knew that. Even Private Harold Bixby.

"I guess I'll come along," Bixby said.

Mack Pierce nodded. He had no taste for this, even with a bastard like Bixby who had ridden down an Indian boy over on the reservation and then shot the boy's father for interfering.

Pierce didn't like executions all the same. He couldn't recall but one other at Fort Lincoln during his tenure, and now they had two within a month of one another.

"You doing all right, Billy?" Mack Pierce asked.

The other figure in the cell was sitting on the bare bunk, pressed against the wall, unmoving. He didn't answer Pierce. Bixby turned back toward the kid and grinned maliciously. "I'll let 'em know you're comin' when I get there," the soldier said. And then he laughed, long and harshly—until the drum roll sounded again. Then he was silent, he wasn't man enough for that.

Mark Pierce bent over and touched the younger prisoner on the shoulder. There was no response at all. Pierce patted the shoulder and then turned, walking out into the corridor where the guards waited to escort Harold Bixby to the parade ground where he would face the firing squad.

The iron door clanged shut. Billy Sondberg lifted his head as he heard it. He saw the men shuffle off down the corridor, toward the outside door of the jailhouse. Beyond the stockade wall the drum roll sounded again and a sob rose up in Billy Sondberg's throat, pressing hot tears from his eyes.

It was a long while before anything happened. Billy sat stiffly, hands clenched together, head up, eyes alert, although he could see nothing of what was happening outside.

When the volley sounded Sondberg felt he had taken the shot. He let out his breath sharply as if someone had driven a fist into his solar plexus, and then he simply slumped over, his shoulder knocking against the cold stone wall.

He lay there, staring at nothing, watching the shadows move across the wall of the cell. There was no way, just none. There was no refuge. Only in sleep, perhaps. If he could sleep—just close his eyes and drift away from reality, from cold, murderous reality. And so he closed his eyes, but sleep was a long, long time in coming.

He awoke before he was ready to, but then it is difficult to stay asleep when someone is tickling you, running her lips along the inside of your thigh, when a mass of red-gold hair is falling across your abdomen and groin.

"Don't you ever sleep, woman?" Ruff Justice asked, and the face of the girl came up to smile at him. She crawled forward, catlike, her full breasts swaying. She gave a contented little sigh and snuggled down on top of the scout.

"I thought you'd wake up."

"And if I hadn't?"

"I would have continued anyway."

"Like that, is it?" he asked, wiping back the hair from her eyes.

"It is this morning, Ruffin."

He kissed her parted lips, then placed his hand behind her neck and kissed her again, harder.

"You wake up fast," she murmured. Her hand slid across Ruff's thigh to his very rapidly awakening groin. She leaned toward him, kissed his throat and then sat up, quickly straddling him, lifting her body, positioning Ruff and sliding onto him with a sharp sigh.

"You don't let a man catch his breath, woman."

"I've never noticed you running out of breath . . . or ambition." She swayed forward and then back, lifting Ruff's hands to place them on her full, nearly round breasts where rosebud nipples stood tautly out.

She smiled very deeply, a sensuous, satisfied smile,

and looked down into the face of the tall, lean man with the dark mustache, the dark hair which curled down past his shoulders. His nose was nearly straight, but the bridge showed a slight curve as if it had been once broken. It had. His mouth was thin, always faintly amused, sometimes cynical. The eyes were ice-cold, blue, knowing, but again the amusement was there. Life had been a grand game to Ruffin T. Justice, but he was aware of the final cosmic joke, his own mortality.

There were scars on his torso, arms, and shoulders. He was a warrior despite the fact that he wrote and read poetry, that he had traveled to Europe with Bill Cody and been entertained by ladies of various courts, that he knew wines—but did not drink them—in a country where raw whiskey and green beer were the rule. There were men who didn't like Ruff Justice, a few that were waiting to meet him again, to have another chance at killing him.

And there were a lot of women waiting to meet him again for entirely different reasons.

All of this Corine knew or read in the eyes of the tall man. Just now she was too busy *feeling* to think. She lifted herself and then slowly settled, her fingers dropping to her crotch to explore herself, to touch Ruff Justice entering her, and she shuddered again.

Ruff lay back watching the morning sun in her copper hair, seeing the concentration on her face, the pleasure behind her sea-green eyes.

Corine was a giving woman, but when she needed to have sex, she took. She worked herself against Ruff, her pelvis gently thumping his, her distant eyes half closed now as the muscles within her altered and loosened and the warmth began to leak from her.

"Ruff . . . damn you, don't hold back," she panted.

He had never wanted to deprive a lady and he didn't start now. Ruff drew her to him and rolled her onto her side. Her right leg lifted and then hooked around him as Ruff arched his back and drove his need home time and again, Corine's fingers running across his lips, down his back, and to his erect shaft as she kissed his hard-muscled chest, his shoulders.

She swayed and pitched against him, cresting a wave of joy as Ruff searched her, striking home again and again, lighting Corine's eyes, bringing her sensitive flesh, her bundles of overexcited nerve endings, to a rushing climax. Ruff held her close to him, his hands clenching her smooth, firm buttocks, letting his own body find its completion.

She breathed in tiny little puffs, stroking his hair, kissing him lightly everywhere her lips could reach as her body spasmed and relaxed.

"Now," she said, "you can sleep."

"Now," he said, "I can't." He began to nudge her, to roll her onto her back, lifting her legs as his lips searched her breasts and throat.

"I want to eat, Ruff. A bath and then breakfast, all right?" She had her arms around his neck. She smiled as he plunged deeper into her body. "Oh, hell . . ." she murmured. "No one's that hungry."

There was a knock at the door and Ruff Justice managed to ignore it completely. He was on his knees now, Corine's heels slung across his shoulders as he drove into her time and again and her body, sweet, warm, once sated, began to come to life again. His fingers went to her crotch and he gently stroked her, spreading her as he sank into her. Her fingers joined his and intertwined, feeling her own dampness.

The knock sounded again on the door and someone softly called, "Mr. Justice."

"Go away," Justice growled, and his hands slid beneath Corine's soft ass, lifting her higher as he swayed against her, seeing her face, beyond the mounds of her smooth white breasts, relax with deep pleasure as he climaxed again, Corine's fingers holding his shaft as he did, encouraging him, demanding more.

Her legs were straight in the air now, spread wide as Ruff again began a slow circular motion, his hands massaging the firm flesh of her breasts.

"Mr. Justice!" The voice from beyond the door was growing insistent. Knuckles rapped on wood.

"I always thought this was a respectable hotel," Ruff growled.

Corine laughed. "Better answer it."

"No."

"It may be important."

"I know it is. Anyone that would come around to disturb me while I'm off duty would have to have an important reason."

"Then?" She touched her fingers to his lips and smiled.

"Don't blame me if you never see me again," Justice grumbled, rolling away from her. "Just a minute!" he shouted at the door. Stepping into his pants, he crossed the room, sweeping back his hair. The hotel clerk in the hallway looked a little nervous, reflecting what he saw in Ruff's eyes.

"The man said to give this to you."

"What man?"

"A soldier." The clerk shrugged. He hesitated as if he actually expected a tip. Ruff closed the door in his face. Corine tittered.

"Now, now," she said. Ruff grunted a reply, walked to the window and opened the note, reading it twice quickly.

He sighed and turned toward Corine.

"Is it important?" she asked, sitting up in bed, pulling a sheet up under her chin.

"Important enough," Ruff answered. The note wasn't real explicit. It was from Mack Pierce. Mack was asking a favor, and it was the only time Ruff could ever recall the big sergeant doing so. If Mack needed a favor, it was important. Pierce was the sort who took pride in doing things himself. He ran that army post with a little help from Colonel MacEnroe.

Mack and Ruff had shared a canteen, a blanket, and a war or two. Justice looked at Corine and shrugged. "Sorry."

"Oh, hell," she said with a short laugh, "you go on and do your soldiering. I'll be here when you get back."

Ruff dressed in buckskins. He fitted a new black hat over his carefully brushed hair, flipped his gunbelt around his waist, picked up his sheathed Spencer .56 repeater and saddlebags, and turned back toward the bed.

"You need any money, Corine?"

"Me? No, what for? I'll let you buy me breakfast, though."

"All right." Ruff left a little gold money on the bureau. She said she didn't need money, but Justice knew she did. That dress shop of hers had folded up flat. When he looked back toward the bed, she was lying there with her head on the pillow—and damn all if the woman wasn't sleeping!

Justice rode his buckskin gelding out toward Fort Lincoln. The Missouri flowed past, cold, silver-blue, swollen with upcountry rain. The fort itself seemed small and dark against the surrounding plains. There were more than the usual amount of civilians there when Ruff arrived.

He had forgotten—there had been a little amusement for them that morning. Harold Bixby. If ever a man had deserved to die it was Bixby. But no man deserved to have his death, a very private matter, turned into a circus.

Ruff rode through the gates, feeling the subdued mood of the soldiers. He swung down at the orderly room, loosely hitched his buckskin horse, and walked inside, slapping the dust from himself.

Mack Pierce wasn't at his desk. That was unusual.

The big man hated to move from his comfortable chair. Rising was a great effort for the first sergeant. Mack tended to remain at rest.

"What's up?" Justice asked the corporal of the guard.

"You want Mack, Mr. Justice?" the kid replied. "He's in with the colonel"

"You want to tell them I'm here?"

"Go on in. They've been waiting a good hour for you."

Justice stepped into the colonel's office, surprised and puzzled by what he found there. Mack Pierce was drinking whiskey. The colonel was drinking it with him. An overstuffed, pleasant-appearing woman was watching them from the corner chair. All three looked around expectantly as Ruff Justice entered the room.

"You sent for me?"

"Yes. Come in, Ruff," Colonel MacEnroe answered. The old man looked worried. His silver mustache seemed to tug his mouth downward. His eyebrows were drawn together. "This is Mrs. Mary Sondberg," he said, gesturing at the woman, and Ruff bowed from the neck.

"How do you do."

The woman seemed unable to answer. Ruff could sense her grief, a grief so deep that perhaps she was afraid to try to speak, fearing the sobs that would emerge. Sergeant Mack Pierce moved toward her, and the huge NCO stood protectively—and a little possessively—by her. A light slowly dawned in Ruff's mind. Damn the old cuss, he had a woman.

"Have we met?" Ruff asked.

"Mrs. Sondberg lives in Bismark," Mack said, answering for her. "Justice has been away. Out in Colorado," Pierce explained to the woman. "He hasn't heard about—well, about things."

The colonel asked, "Would you like to go out and get a little air while we discuss matters, Mrs. Sondberg?"

"No, sir," she said, managing to speak rather firmly. "I would like to hear this. I've stood a lot, I reckon I can stand a little more. Please, Mr. Justice, don't stand on my account."

Justice pulled up a chair and had a seat, balancing his hat on his knee as he sat waiting.

The colonel began it. "You know we had an execution this morning, Ruff. Damnable affairs. I don't like them."

"Yes, sir. I heard about that down in town."

"Did you know we have another scheduled for next month?"

"No, I didn't. Who?"

"His name is Billy Sondberg." The woman choked off a little sob, and Ruff's eyes flickered that way. "Yes, this is his mother."

"Desertion?" Ruff asked.

"Desertion!" That got the woman stirred up. "Billy would never desert the army. He loves it. Ever since he was a little boy and first saw Mack in his dress uniform—Sergeant Pierce," she amended, looking away briefly.

"I practically talked the kid into enlisting," Mack said, and his red, flaccid face looked tormented.

"No, you never did, Mack." The woman took his meaty hand briefly. "He always wanted to join."

"I used to go to visit on Sundays," Mack said to no one. "Mary would fry chicken and serve me lemonade. I'd sit on the porch glider telling Billy tales about the Indians and all—most of 'em were true." He smiled crookedly.

"It's murder, Ruff," Colonel MacEnroe said quietly. "The kid has been found guilty of murdering a young settler woman. And unless you can find some proof that he didn't do it, he's going to face a firing squad on the fifteenth of next month."

The woman broke down then and wept openly. Mack Pierce, looking awkward and weary, draped a huge arm over her shoulder. MacEnroe smothered a curse and turned sharply away, while the tall man in buckskins sat listening, watching, wondering just what in hell they expected him to be able to do about it. And across the post a kid of eighteen sat in a dark stone cell counting out the last hours of his life.

JOIN THE RUFF JUSTICE READERS' PANEL

Help us bring you more of the books you like by filling out this survey and mailing it in today.

1. Book title:_____

   Book #:_____

2. Using the scale below how would you rate this book on the following features.

Poor		Not so Good			O.K.			Good		Excellent
0	1	2	3	4	5	6	7	8	9	10

	Rating
Overall opinion of book	_____
Plot/Story	_____
Setting/Location	_____
Writing Style	_____
Character Development	_____
Conclusion/Ending	_____
Scene on Front Cover	_____

3. On average about how many western books do you buy for yourself each month?_____

4. How would you classify yourself as a reader of westerns?
   I am a ( ) light ( ) medium ( ) heavy reader.

5. What is your education?
   ( ) High School (or less)   ( ) 4 yrs. college
   ( ) 2 yrs. college   ( ) Post Graduate

6. Age_____   7. Sex: ( ) Male ( ) Female

Please Print Name_____

Address_____

City_____State_____Zip_____

Phone # (   )_____

Thank you. Please send to New American Library, Research Dept, 1633 Broadway, New York, NY 10019.

SIGNET Westerns You'll Enjoy by Leo P. Kelley

(0451)